A rising wind was swishing in the curtains—or was it a rustling outside the door that she could hear?

The door handle *was* turning!

Meg scarcely breathed as the door opened. She wanted to call out, "Who is it?" but ridiculously she had lost her voice. She lay petrified, watching a shadowy form appear.

A man? A woman?

There seemed to be no face, just an indistinguishable paleness.

A head like an egg, smooth and white.

It was then that Meg began to scream. . . .

Dorothy Eden

Face of an Angel

writing under the name of MARY PARADISE

ace books

A Division of Grosset & Dunlap, Inc.
1120 Avenue of the Americas
New York, New York 10036

It was five years since Meg had been to the villa outside Florence. The sun shone just as hotly, the olive trees were parched to a drab green in the brilliant light, and the rooftops of Florence in the distance had their tawny eternal color. The only change that had taken place was to the villa itself.

Five years ago it had been derelict enough, a forlorn home for a young girl, but now, to Meg's dismay, she saw that it was ruined and abandoned. The windows gaped, part of the roof had fallen in and the weeds had grown even taller round the flaked and pitted walls.

One could not be surprised as, badly scarred and damaged by the war, the villa had threatened to topple into ruins ever since. But what had happened to Angelica?

When Meg had met her on her last holiday in Florence she had been living with her grandmother in the three or four least damaged rooms. She was just sixteen, and scarcely remembered the war, except as the bewildering time when her parents and her only brother had been killed, and only she and her grandmother had escaped. The old lady, full of fanatical pride and devotion to the past, had, in spite of abject poverty, tried to bring Angelica up in the traditions of a high-class family, but the question of her future had become an intense worry. She was going to be beautiful. Had it been before the war there would have been no difficulty about arranging a good marriage for her. But everything had changed. Angelica had no parents, no money, only a derelict villa and a half crazy grandmother. She was a shy enchanting creature just ready to step out into the world.

Meg, the young English girl, happening in by chance, partly to ask the shortest way back to the city, partly to explore the strange ghostly house, had been welcomed with the greatest courtesy, and eventually invited to stay the night. Angelica spoke very little English, but the old grandmother was fluent. Meg was only three years older than Angelica. The old lady made searching inquiries as to what, in this new strange world, a sheltered girl of good family could do. Angelica was running wild, like a peasant. She should be going to balls and parties. But she had no clothes. She was dressed in what was little more than rags. Her existence was one of the most spartan simplicity.

Meg remembered drinking tart red wine and eating cheese and listening to the old woman with the parchment face and glittering eyes, and watching the shy girl. With that pale oval face, smooth dark hair and beautifully slender body she could have been a model, perhaps a film star. Probably she would end by getting a poorly paid respectable job in one of the art galleries or tourists departments. Meg had tried to give practical advice, though at that time she was romantically dazed by the glory of Florence and kept thinking of this slender girl walking through a Medici palace, dressed in wonderful clothes.

What had happened to Angelica she had never heard, and now, when at last she had the opportunity to find out, she was faced with an empty and abandoned house.

Not quite abandoned, for suddenly, as Meg turned away, an old man emerged from a derelict shed at the back of the house. He called sharply, asking Meg what she wanted. She summoned up her faulty Italian enough to ask where Angelica was. The old grandmother presumably was dead. But where was Angelica and what had happened to the house?

It had been struck by lightning, he answered. Suddenly one night in a storm the roof fell in. But there had been no one living there then. Angelica had married and her grandmother had, as Meg had guessed, died.

"Who did Angelica marry?" Meg asked, thinking of the quiet serene beauty of the girl, waiting to spring into radiant life at the right touch.

"A rich Englishman." The old man smiled with satisfaction, crinkling his walnut face. "The little signorina did well for herself after all."

The Englishman had apparently come accidentally to the villa, much as Meg had done, seen Angelica who was then nineteen, and fallen in love immediately. The wedding had taken place very quickly because the old grandmother had not much longer to live. And that was fortunate for everyone, for shortly afterwards the storm had struck and the tottering old house had met its doom.

"Do you remember the Englishman's name?" Meg was anxious that the girl, her friend of those few enchanted days, was happy. And one never knew, she might be able to trace her whereabouts in England.

He was connected with art, the old man answered. He had come to Florence to visit the galleries. He was rich and cultured. His name? It was a foreign one. Something like Wilton. Claudius Wilton? The wedding had been very quiet, no one but the priest, the old grandmother and a friend of Signor Wilton's.

Meg thanked the old man and tucked the name away in her memory. Mrs. Claude Wilton, who was now a rich young woman probably able to buy pictures of her own. It seemed a fairytale ending for the quiet little girl with her budding beauty, and her background of tragedy. Meg decided that she must make every endeavor to find her again, if only to look at her photograph in society papers. Derek was connected with the art world. He might know of Claude Wilton. How happy the grandmother must have been to know that after all little Angelica had made a suitable marriage. . . .

Back in London Meg plunged back into her own private unhappiness. She had known for a long time that Derek was not serious. She had gone abroad in an endeavor to grow out of a love affair that was daily causing her more pain. She had only been away for three weeks. It was foolish to think that in that time Derek might have missed her enough to be waiting impatiently on her doorstep.

He wasn't of course. She spent the first evening back in the old pattern of waiting for the telephone to ring. and standing at the window until it was too dark to see, hoping the tall familiar figure might appear down the street. He had forgotten the day of her return, although she had sent him that casual postcard. Perhaps he had deliberately forgotten. He had been hinting for some time that much as he loved her, he did not intend to settle down for several years. Meg didn't even mind waiting several years, provided they stayed in love. But deep inside herself she knew that Derek wouldn't. He wasn't in love even now. Or he would have met her or sent flowers, or telephoned.

Meg blinked her eyes. She was determined not to cry. It was nauseatingly self-pitying to sit all alone crying for something that had happened and couldn't be mended. She mustn't show she was hurt. Above all, she mustn't cling.

To divert herself she picked up the telephone book and began looking up the Wiltons. If the Claude Wiltons lived in London she would telephone and ask to speak to Angelica. It would be amusing and interesting. She wondered how well Angelica now spoke English, and how much confidence marriage had brought into her secret little face.

But there was no Claude Wilton listed. That meant that the couple probably lived in the country, fashionably far from London. There was, however, the Wilton Galleries in Grosvenor Street. Would that be Claude's business? Could she ring in the morning and ask if a Claude Wilton was there?

This was growing a little like a detective story. If the Wiltons were very grand, of course, they mightn't want a girl with a humble secretarial job claiming friendship. Although Angelica, Meg was certain, would not be like that.

Just as she was drawing the curtains to shut out the last of the dusk the telephone did ring.

Meg drew a deep breath. She looked round the familiar room, thinking that if she were really to part from Derek she would have to move, for there was too much here that they had shared, the amusing

wall paper with the spotted red and white mush-
rooms, the two table lamps they had found in a junk
shop, the impractical white rugs that Derek had said
were *chi chi*. . . .

All this flashed through her mind as she picked
up the receiver and heard his familiar voice.

"Hullo, darling. Had a wonderful time? Sorry I
couldn't get to meet you. I was heavily involved."

He didn't say what in, and Meg realized that she
had got past the happy confident days of being able
to ask frankly what he had been doing.

"Where are you now?"

"I'm home. I've had quite a day. When do you
go back to the office?"

"Next Monday. Why?"

"I've got an invitation to a preview of an art exhibition tomorrow." Meg's heart leapt. That would
mean lunch, an hour at the show, an early escape
to wander across the park. Bliss. . . .

But Derek was going on, "I can't go myself. I'm
tied up. But you might like to use the invitation.
Fresh from Florence, your appetite's probably whet-
ted."

Meg swallowed her disappointment.

"Or satiated," she said coolly. "I don't think I
could make it, thanks. I've an awful lot to do."

"Oh, have you? A pity. It's at the Wilton Galleries."

"What!" She felt a tremor go over her, a feeling
of predestination, or fate.

"Does that interest you?" Derek was asking.

"A little. Just a coincidence. Is the owner a Claude
Wilton?"

"No. Clive. Do you know him? A suave fellow.
I'm never sure about him."

Clive was near enough to Claude or Claudius, as the old man had said. He had probably made a mistake with the foreign name.

"Did he marry an Italian girl?" Meg asked, controlling her excitement.

"I know nothing about his private life. He is married, I believe. What's the matter, darling? You sound as if you've found a long lost friend."

"I think I may have. I knew his wife when she was a girl living near Florence. The barefoot contessa sort of thing. I believe I'd like to use that invitation after all."

"Then it's yours. I'll put it in the mail."

"Oh." She had had a forlorn hope that he might bring it over. "When shall I see you?"

"When I get out of this mad whirl." Belatedly he asked, "How are you looking?"

"Oh—sunburnt."

"Don't lose it all before I see you. Good night, sweetie. Enjoy the Italian contessa."

II

Meg mingled with the smart crowds, taking only a cursory glance at the pictures. She was looking for Angelica's sweet calm face, sure that she must be there, marveling at the astonishing fact that her search should be so simple. The old grandmother would have said it was the hand of fate leading the two girls together again.

Because Derek was not to be there, Meg had taken little trouble over her own appearance. She wore a short-sleeved linen dress and her long fair hair was twisted into a casual swirl at the back of her head. Apart from the sophisticated simplicity of her dress she looked much as she had done when she had first met Angelica.

But it didn't seem that Angelica was here, after all. Meg threaded her way disappointedly through the crowd. It was a few minutes before she realized that, just as she was looking for Angelica, someone seemed to be looking for her. Surely that small thick-set man with the curiously ravaged face was staring at her intently. She moved away, strangely uneasy. Why should someone stare at her like that? She seemed to have lost the man in the crowd, and breathed more easily. Then, a moment later, she started as someone took her arm. Looking round, she saw that it was the same odd man with the fixed dark stare.

"Forgive me, but I must speak to you," he said in a slow deep voice that had a foreign accent. "You look just like a Botticelli angel."

Meg laughed uneasily, wondering how to cope with the little man's unconventional and excited approach.

"Oh, I think you're exaggerating—"

"I'm not exaggerating at all. Clive!" The extraordinary person was beckoning to someone else. "Clive, come here!"

A little distance away a man turned. He was slender, tall, with dark intensely bright eyes. His face was vaguely but attractively monkeyish, full of animation and alertness. Meg's heart was beating rapidly. So this was Clive Wilton, the man who had married the charming youthful Angelica. She had

8

wanted to meet him, but not in quite such unusual circumstances, with herself the object of attention.

"Clive, here's a young lady with the face of an angel."

Clive Wilton came rather quickly then, as if he were disturbed. No heavenly visitors for Clive Wilton, Meg thought intuitively. He had no time for anything but the present very earthly moment. That was evident in every line of his impatient restless body.

"I don't know her name," the short man went on, "but isn't it true? She's a Botticelli angel."

Meg was puzzled and more than a little embarrassed by his excitement. She hadn't known artists behaved like this. She thought a little explanation was due.

"My name's Margaret Burney," she said, speaking to Clive Wilton. "I'm not exactly a guest here. I'm Derek Moore's friend, but he couldn't come so he gave me his invitation card. I'm awfully pleased to meet you, Mr. Wilton, because I think I know your wife."

Was that a flash of something more than surprise in Clive Wilton's dark eyes?

"My wife?" He spoke in a clipped sharp voice.

"Yes. I met her in Florence in that tumbledown villa where she and her grandmother lived. That was five years ago. But when I went back last week to see if they were still there I found the house abandoned."

"I'm afraid I don't know who you're talking about, Miss Burney." Clive Wilton's voice was quite polite, but cold and impersonal. "My wife came from Rome."

9

"Not Angelica?" Meg was sharply disappointed. She hadn't realized how interested she had been in seeing Angelica again.

"Her name is Luisa. You must be talking of someone else."

"But the old man said Angelica had married an Englishman. Someone connected with art. A Claudius Wilton. I took that to be Claude, which really isn't very different from Clive, is it?"

Meg's bewilderment had made her speak emphatically. She didn't notice at once the quick nervous drawing together of the man's thin dark eyebrows.

"He has the names confused, obviously. Or perhaps you didn't understand his accent. Claudius." He gave a faint smile. "That flatters me. Eh, Hans? I'm scarcely an emperor. But I do have a small empire here which I must look after. You'll excuse me, Miss Burney?"

He moved away. At the same moment, whether by accident or intention, Meg noticed a broad-shouldered young man with heavy untidy tawny hair and casual clothes watching her. His brown eyes held admiration, or was it inquisitive interest, as if he had deliberately overheard her conversation. As he noticed her become aware of him he turned away.

Meg scarcely heard what the short dark man was saying until his last words jerked her into full consciousness.

"You must forgive Clive, Miss Burney. He does have an Italian wife who came from Rome. But it upsets him to talk of her. She's in the hospital, very ill."

"Oh, I'm sorry."

"Perhaps your informant mixed the Englishmen's names. He probably hadn't heard many before. He would be a countryman."

"He was a peasant. It wasn't likely he would hear of a marriage as far away as Rome."

"He may have. It was talked of a lot. Luisa came from a good family. She was very beautiful."

"Was?"

"She's ill now, poor thing. Chronically ill." The man shook his head, his face settling into tragic lines. "So perhaps your little Angelica with her husband, whoever he is, is the happiest."

Meg was silent a moment, still puzzled. Could she have mistaken the name the old man had told her? Or could he have made a mistake? Was it likely that so sophisticated and successful a man as Clive Wilton appeared to be would marry a little ragged girl out of a tumbledown house, even though she showed her promise of beauty?

"I'm Hans Cromer," said the man beside her. "These are my paintings. Not good you say? I know myself they're not. But Clive is my friend. He's good enough to hang one or two."

Meg looked at the simple water colors. Attractive enough, certainly. They would make pretty calendars. They were scarcely the kind of thing to be hung at a smart exhibition of fashionable moderns.

"What I really want to do," the little man sighed, "is to paint portraits. It is like the thin man trying to get out of the fat one. He never does. But he keeps on trying. I fear I am a failure."

"Oh, no, Mr. Cromer." Meg didn't know why she should hear this confession, but she was a sympathetic person, and was distressed by the man's sad

11

resignation. He had gentle dark brown eyes and a beaten look. His past was probably a shadow over him, as Angelica's had been.

"Yes. And it is only Clive's wonderful friendship that enables me to survive. We are neighbors, you see. We live in the same village. That's why I feel so much for Clive with his poor sweet wife."

"Has she been in the hospital for a long time?"

"For months, yes. Clive lives with a housekeeper, in that beautiful house. Luisa was such a decoration to it."

"Is she going to die?" Meg asked.

"Oh, no, not die."

A dark look had come and gone fleetingly in the man's face. Some other people were crowding round to look at the pictures, and someone else spoke to him. Meg moved a little away, watching Clive Wilton's sleek dark head. So he, for all his apparent confidence in life, had tragedy, too. She was beginning to wish she hadn't come. Her own depression was returning. Her hunch about Angelica had been wrong, and she wasn't really interested in modern paintings. She knew nothing about techniques, and only enough generally to be surprised at the incongruity of Hans Cromer's pretty water colors hanging on these walls. Clive must really be a good friend.

"You're interested in art, Miss Burney?"

Meg started as she realized Clive Wilton was beside her, and looking at her with his bright skeptical eyes. His voice was skeptical, too. She suspected that he wasn't particularly pleased to have her, a person who knew little about art, cluttering up his smart gallery on someone else's invitation. He wanted only people who would be of use to him, or whom he could impress.

And he hadn't liked the questions about his wife.

She had been clumsy, of course. But she didn't know that his wife was so ill.

"Mr. Cromer was telling me about your wife's illness," she said impulsively. "I'm so sorry. It must be a great worry for you."

"She is recovering," he said briefly. "I hope you will find your friend, Miss Burney."

"Angelica? Yes. I haven't a clue about her now. I was so sure it must be you she'd married. But the coincidence would have been too extraordinary. To have heard of her husband one day, and to meet him the next."

"Yes. It would have been too extraordinary. Life isn't like that."

It was an unsatisfactory little conversation. Meg was convinced that for some reason Clive Wilton had formed a dislike for her. She was too brash and impulsive. He would like extremely sophisticated women. That was one reason why it really was unlikely that he would have married simple little Angelica with her halting English. But there was another more puzzling thing. He hadn't liked being asked about his wife. Because she was ill? Or because he preferred, in these smart gatherings, to forget her existence?

She noticed that the broad-shouldered young man with the untidy hair was watching her again. This time there was no doubt that he was interested in her. He seemed about to come over and speak, but, evading any more conversation with strangers, Meg slipped into the cloakroom. When she came out a little later she heard lowered voices in the foyer. One of them was Hans Cromer's. Unobserved, she stood behind the half-opened door and listened.

"You've had enough, don't you think?" The impatient clipped quality was Clive Wilton's voice again. "You surely can manage without this?"

"Not when such an opportunity presents itself. You must see that."

"But the risk—"

"Ah, it is negligible. Like the others. Let us deal with that if and when it arises."

"No!" Clive said sharply. "It isn't negligible. This might be once too often This might be the time when you stick your neck out too far."

"But you don't understand, my dear Clive. It will make all the difference. It's what I've been waiting for. It gives me the final inspiration. I simply can't afford not to have it. Besides, under the circumstances, wouldn't it be better—"

The voices moved further away. Meg caught the words, ". . . knows too much," and that was all.

When she came into view the two men had moved back into the gallery.

It was raining outside, a sharp sudden thundershower that was drenching in its intensity. Meg had been foolish enough to come without coat or umbrella. The day had been so fine that she had absently been thinking of the reliable Italian weather.

She stood uncertainly at the door pondering her chance of getting a taxi. She didn't notice that she had been joined by the young man who had previously been watching her, until he spoke.

"The doorman's getting me a taxi," he said. "Can I give you a lift?"

Meg had the odd feeling that he had watched to see when she left and had deliberately followed her. But surely this couldn't be so since already the doorman had been dispatched, beneath his large umbrella, to the corner. Nevertheless, anything could happen on this strange afternoon. Even the rain was adding to its complexities.

"I expect it will stop soon," she said.

"Not this downpour. It will go on for an hour. And you haven't even got a hat."

"Silly of me," Meg murmured.

"I'm going to Chelsea. Can I drop you anywhere en route? Am I wrong but, you look like South Kensington to me?"

Meg looked at him and decided that he was to be trusted, more or less. There was remarkably little guile in his steady eyes.

"Drayton Gardens," she said. "I would be awfully grateful for a lift since it's on your way."

"It's a pleasure. I believe this is my taxi now. You must be cold." He was looking at her bare arms.

She smiled involuntarily. "I am a little, but what do you propose to do about that?"

"We could sit closer than is customary with strangers."

He opened the door for her to get in, and gave instructions to the driver. Then he got in beside her, smiling. He was older than he had seemed on first sight, his face deeply creased, and flecks of premature grey at his temples.

"We don't have to be strangers, of course. I'm Simon Somers."

"And you know who I am," Meg answered coolly. "Because you overheard the conversation I had with Mr. Wilton. Or am I making a mistake?"

15

"Touché," said Simon. "I'm flattered that you noticed me. I was thinking how you lit up the place, and naturally I tried to hear your voice, too."

"Was that all?" Everything, now, seemed suspicious. "You're not on this angel business, too?"

"Angel?" He was looking at her intently, his eyes strangely unamused.

"I just met a crazy artist, Hans Cromer. Do you know him?"

"Yes, I do. I come from the same village."

Meg turned interestedly, forgetting her suspicion, although this was another coincidence.

"Do you really?"

"Yes, Frenchley. On the Kent coast. Clive Wilton lives there, too. That's how I happened to be at his exhibition. I was in London selling a pair of Meissen figures at Sotheby's. I thought I'd look in on Clive."

"Then you'll know his wife. Do tell me what she's like."

His brows went up. "And why this deep interest in another man's wife?"

"Because I think I've met her. Oh, it's nothing to do with Clive Wilton personally. I couldn't care less if he has six wives. But although he says she isn't I still get this feeling she's Angelica."

She saw his look of bewilderment, and explained, "That's a girl I met in Italy five years ago. When I was there again last week I heard she'd married a rich Englishman interested in the arts. But Clive said his wife wasn't Angelica."

"Her name's Luisa. She's certainly Italian, and more I can't tell you as I've never seen her."

"Never seen her! But you said you live in the same village."

"Clive and his wife had only just moved there at

16

the time of her accident. The poor girl's been in the hospital ever since."

"Then hadn't anyone seen her?"

"Not the locals, no. Hans Cromer had, of course. He's an intimate friend."

"How tragic for Mr. Wilton," Meg said.

"Is it?"

"What do you mean?"

"It's tragic for the girl, Luisa, Angelica whoever she is," Simon said levelly. "But Clive has his way of finding compensations. He admires a pretty girl. Didn't you notice the way he looked at you?"

Meg looked at him coldly. "On the contrary, he scarcely looked at me at all! And what he saw he didn't appear to like."

"Oh, Clive's subtle. Much more subtle than poor old Hans who is only an artists. Or me, for instance."

He spoke the truth. There was nothing subtle about the admiration in his eyes.

"It's very kind of you to share your taxi," Meg said stiffly. "But let's leave it at that."

He leaned forward. "I had a foolish optimistic hope that you'd have dinner with me tonight."

"I have an engagement, I'm sorry."

"Have you really? And are you sorry?"

Meg nodded, thinking of Derek who might or might not bother to ring her. In any case, why couldn't a simple ride in a taxi on a rainy afternoon remain at that?

"Oh, too bad. I suppose it was too much to hope for. I've neither money nor looks."

"What *are* you talking about? You're a stranger."

"I'd rather not be, you know. I'd very much like to be your friend. Shall I see you again?"

"I shouldn't think it's at all likely," Meg said coldly.

"Not even if Clive Wilton remembers your pretty face?"

Again he puzzled her with his unexpected statement that seemed to have some underlying meaning.

"I don't know what you're talking about. If you're trying to tell me something please do it in language that I understand."

"All right, then. Much as I'd like to see you in Frenchley, keep away from Clive. It's like playing with a live electric wire."

Meg was completely bewildered, but again that strange not unpleasant shiver of excitement went over her. Her life had been getting dull and unsatisfactory, and this was something happening. Or almost happening.

"I can't think what you mean. I never expect to see Clive Wilton again."

"You're probably right," Simon said mildly. "I've got an off-beat sort of imagination. Janie will tell you."

"Janie?"

"Janie Howard. You'll meet her if you come to Frenchley. But you don't need to be jealous of her. She thinks she's in love with Hans, not Clive."

The taxi had swung around a corner.

"This is where I get out," Meg said in some relief. "I don't understand a word of what you've been saying, and I think you're rather impertinent. But it was kind of you to give me a lift. I hope you find some girl who understands you to have dinner with you tonight."

"Oh, I'll eat with my mother," Simon said resignedly. "She likes the opportunity to lecture me. She's seriously afraid women don't like me."

"With some justification," Meg retorted.

Simon grinned. "I'll be seeing you, all the same. Like to take a bet on it? But I almost wish you hadn't such a lovely face. Beauty can be dangerous. Did you know?"

And again, although his voice was light, there was that unamused look in his eyes.

Derek did ring that evening. Meg's heart gave its familiar leap of pleasure. She steeled herself to show indifference.

"Hi, darling! I hear you made a hit today."

"Whoever with? That funny little foreigner who paints bad water colors?"

"No. With the maestro himself."

Meg had a strong feeling of excitement, mingled with apprehension. Had Simon been right after all?

"Derek, don't be absurd. He didn't even like me. I asked some clumsy questions about his wife, and made a frightful *faux pas*. He thought I was just inquisitive—as I was."

Derek laughed. "You didn't remind him of the time when his wife went barefoot?"

"It wasn't that wife—I mean that girl. Although oddly enough he did marry an Italian. It's all rather mystifying, but I don't suppose I shall ever know the answer now."

"You'll have every chance to, my sweet. He's been asking for your telephone number."

"Not Clive Wilton!"

"Don't you love me still?"

"What on earth has that to do with it?"

"I thought I detected excitement in your voice."

"Surprise," said Meg calmly. "Well, even interest, I suppose. If Clive Wilton wants to see me, it must be for some ulterior motive."

"Darling don't you ever look at your face in the mirror? Haven't I told you you're the most beautiful girl in London?"

Derek hadn't paid her compliments for a long time. At least that was something that Clive Wilton had indirectly done for her, she thought cynically.

"Tell me quickly, Derek. I've been doing nothing but get into odd conversations today. What is it this man wants of me?"

"I haven't a clue. To take you to lunch, I think."

"Oh."

"Will you go?"

"Of course. Never refuse a good meal," Meg said flippantly.

"He also asked a lot of questions as to who you were and what you did, what your qualifications were, where your family was."

"But why, Derek?" Meg was serious now, and genuinely puzzled.

"I should think he's probably planning to groom you for his secretary—or his mistress."

If Derek expected her to laugh at that witticism, he was disappointed.

"How well do you know Clive Wilton? I mean, personally?"

"Not at all. I've met him only in business. He's one of these astute young men who's suddenly making a name for himself as an art dealer. I should think he's pretty ambitious, and, as you saw, socially brilliant. But I know nothing of him otherwise."

"Did his wife ever go to his parties? I mean, before she was ill."

"I wouldn't know that either. I don't think he gave parties until recently. If you mean, did she burst on London as a foreign beauty, no, she didn't. But why don't you ask Clive these questions yourself?"

Meg gripped the receiver. "Derek, when am I to see you?"

She hadn't meant to ask. The words had squeezed through her assumed indifference. She kept visualizing his face at the other end of the telephone, wearing its faint hint of alarm whenever she got too serious.

"I've got to go to the Browne's for the weekend. I'm sorry, sweetie. What about dinner next Tuesday? We might take in a film."

"Don't you mind my seeing Clive Wilton, whatever his intentions?"

"Of course I do. I loathe it. But you know what we agreed—no strings. Meg, my pet, I do love you. Be good."

Meg put down the receiver slowly. It was absurd to think that Derek had abandoned her to some unknown danger. She was simply being fanciful.

When Clive Wilton rang the next morning she assumed a look of animation and pleasure, as if he could see her at the other end of the telephone, and said why, yes, she'd love to lunch. What a surprise. She hadn't thought he would remember her.

His voice on the telephone was low and deliberate with a curiously stirring quality What was it that impertinent young man, Simon Somers, had said? That he was like a live electric wire. The simile seemed remarkably apt.

"You underestimate yourself, Miss Burney. I've been looking for someone like you for a long time.

21

Though I'm afraid this is just a business proposition I have to make. I hope you will agree to it. Shall we say the Château Bleu at one next Wednesday?"

III

There was a new nurse on, one Luisa hadn't seen before. She had a soft, pretty face and a kind voice. She was also thoughtful enough to speak slowly so that Luisa could understand her. The other nurse never had time or forgot to enunciate clearly with the result that Luisa never knew what, was happening or what she was supposed to do.

She would tell Clive not to give her a present when she left the hospital.

When she left. . . .

No one would ever tell her when she was to leave. Doctor Lennox simply said: "You mustn't worry, my dear Mrs. Wilton. All this takes time."

And the old nurse said in her brisk unsympathetic way: "Always impatient, dear. How old are you? Twenty-one? My, if I was twenty-one I wouldn't mind keeping my husband waiting for a while. Plenty of time for *that* still."

This comment Luisa didn't understand, but it must have been meant to be funny, for the younger nurse snickered and didn't meet Luisa's eyes.

Clive himself, on his brief visits, would not commit himself at all. "It's not in my hands, darling. You must trust the doctor."

"Clive, I can't stay here for months, for years."

"Of course you won't have to. Silly angel. And remember, you are lucky to be alive."

Lucky? Everyone told her that so often. She supposed she ought to believe them. But how did they know? Heaven might have been much better than this, lying in a hospital bed week after week, waiting for Clive's visits or his letters, searching his face when he came, listening to every inflection of his voice, wondering until she tortured herself how much she trusted him.

The new nurse, obviously wanting to cheer her up, told her that Doctor Lennox was very pleased with her.

"Does he say when I can go home?" Luisa asked eagerly.

"Actually he did say a spell out of the hospital before your next operation might do you good. But that depended—"

"Depended?"

The nurse looked a little alarmed, as if she was afraid she had said too much.

"Well, on your home circumstances, Mrs. Wilton."

Luisa said quite calmly, "You mean whether my husband wants me or not?"

"Oh, Mrs. Wilton!" The girl's pretty face was shocked. "What a thing to say! He adores you. Everyone knows that. Look at your flowers. Fresh ones every day. And letters. In fact, I've got a letter for you now. I'll leave it with you when I've done your treatment. It will cheer you up."

This girl was kind. Luisa decided she would ask Clive to get a bracelet for her. A gold charm one that jingled. Young girls liked things that jingled. She did herself. And she was young, too. Only twenty-one.

Clive wouldn't object to buying the bracelet when it was for someone else. It was only she whom he didn't like having jewelry. Not the ostentatious kind, anyway. A lady didn't make herself conspicuous, he said. But he seemed to enjoy seeing pretty pieces of jewelry on other women.

"There, that doesn't hurt, does it?" The nurse was talking to distract Luisa's attention from the pain. "You're coming on beautifully. Your husband won't know you when he sees you next. When will he be down again?"

"I don't know. He's had an important exhibition in London. If it was a success he said it might go on for some time." Luisa, by determined concentration, had taught herself to speak perfect English. All she had to remember was to speak slowly, so that now all her remarks seemed deliberate and measured. "He is very anxious for it to be a success," she added.

"But everything your husband did would be a success, wouldn't it?" the nurse said. "He looks that type."

"He is very ambitious, yes," Luisa murmured.

"What an exciting life you're going to have when you're better. I wish I could meet someone like your husband. Where did you find him, Mrs. Wilton?"

"In Rome. It was a very hot day." Luisa smiled reminiscently. "We were both walking in the Borghese gardens. He asked me to have coffee with him."

"You mean he picked you up!"

"Is that a bad thing?" Luisa was momentarily happy, thinking of that brilliant day, and the Englishman with the ardent eyes who kept looking at her. She had been very young and lonely and sad.

24

She thought she would have talked to anybody, and it was lucky that the first man who had attempted to talk to her had been so charming and so full of integrity. She couldn't believe what was happening to her. It had seemed too good to be true.

"Doesn't seem like a bad thing in your case, does it?" the nurse said brightly. "It couldn't have had a happier ending. Unless, of course, he has a habit of going about picking up pretty girls. Now don't look like that, Mrs. Wilton. I was only joking."

Luisa endeavored to smile. There was no point in telling this nice sympathetic girl what things had been like recently. She must just remember that she had married too young, and with too much innocence. As she grew older she would manage better. She would learn to trust Clive more, or to shut her eyes, as a wise woman would. She would also overcome this constant shadow of fear that hung over her. That, at least, was imaginary, if Clive's reluctance to have her with him in London and at social functions was not.

"There," said the nurse briskly. "That's done for one more time." She was gathering up her things to leave the room.

Luisa grasped her arm. "Nurse, tell me the truth. Have I changed much?"

"I didn't see you before you were ill, Mrs. Wilton. But I'd say, hardly at all. You've got pretty thin, of course, but that can be remedied."

"I will get better? Really better?"

"Doctor Lennox says so. I heard him myself."

Luisa's eyes filled with tears. She was intensely grateful to this nice girl with her charming gentle face. She must ask Clive to buy that bracelet, a really good one, shining gold and pretty. Like the one that someone had left on the side of the wash-basin in a restaurant cloakroom one day, and had come back exclaiming anxiously just as she had picked it up. She always remembered that one, but Clive hadn't cared much for it when she had described it, and had said he would rather see her wearing a good brooch. Which he duly bought for her, and which she duly wore, to please him, but which she found extremely dull and old-fashioned.

"Now I'll leave you to read your letter," the nurse said. "I expect it's to say your husband's coming down any day."

"Perhaps it will say I can go home," Luisa whispered, but not loud enough for the departing nurse to hear. She was too deeply sensitive about it to admit to anyone that she was almost certain Clive didn't want her home.

The letter began as Clive's always did:

"Darling Angel,

"When you receive this I hope you are feeling much brighter and happier than you were the last time I saw you. The doctor says there is no reason for you not to be, so be a good girl and believe him. I am sending you some more books, which I hope will entertain and amuse you, one a new one on Rome—but don't let it make you homesick. The exhibition has been quite a success, though perhaps not so many sales as I had hoped. Still, it has aroused comment, and that is the important thing. I have my eyes on a larger gallery in Bond Street, but that will come with patience.

"I'm sorry all this work has kept me so long in London. But the exhibition closes next week and then I shall be home for quite a spell. I'll be able to visit you every day—if you promise not to let my visits make you sad, as you were doing. That makes us both unhappy, and I feel then that it's better if I stay away. But I've said all this before, and I'm sure you are well enough now to trust me and the doctor and everyone else to be telling you the truth.

"I will be glad to get home for some clean sea air. It has been very hot and dry and dusty in London.

"By the way, I have at last found the kind of girl I have been looking for for a long time, to train as my assistant. Temporarily she will work as my secretary until I have taught her enough to act as receptionist at the gallery and hostess at my exhibitions and business parties. She has, I think, the right manner and looks, but only time will tell. I expect she will marry someone within six months, although she assures me with the greatest emphasis that she will not. Her name is Margaret Burney, and she is twenty-four. I think you will like her, and she will make a pleasant companion for you when you eventually come home—that is, of course, when I don't require her in London.

"I am bringing her down with me next Monday, and if it interests you, will later bring her to the hospital to meet you. She is a pleasant little thing with good intelligence, and I think will be a success. At least she can't be any worse than the terrible Miss Jones. Don't you agree?

"No more now. I'll arrive too late on Monday to come to see you, but at the earliest possible moment the next day. Good-bye, angel. A thousand kisses,

Your Clive."

She must remember, Luisa thought irrelevantly, to tell Clive not to go on calling her angel. The name now was bitterly unsuitable. Or too suitable?

But this girl coming, the one of whom he told her at length but in that deliberately impersonal way. . . .

Luisa's fingers tightened round the letter angrily. At least he hadn't had the previous girl in the house. She was in the village, safely ensconced in the library, knowing very little about books, but keeping her job because Clive knew how to persuade people to do as he wished. Janie Howard. Looking at people with that tip-tilted smile on her charming naughty medieval face.

There had been no need for Clive to tell Luisa whether the new girl, Margaret Burney, was pretty or not. She must be, or he wouldn't have ambitious plans for her.

Luisa lay quietly, her eyes darkened with anger and resentment. It was convenient for Clive to have her here, helpless in a nursing home for a long time. Much too convenient. He relied on her meekly submitting to the doctor's and nurses' and his own wishes.

Perhaps he did love her, really. He said so often enough. But he had other plans, too, in which she was meant to have no part.

Why should she let that happen? She was his wife still. Even disfigured and no longer attractive she had her place in his life to defend. She wouldn't lie here helplessly while another woman, young and attractive, came into her house.

Clive could go too far. He relied too much on her timidity and unsureness, and on her previous blind devotion to him.

Then perhaps it was time to show him she was not so timid. Could she manage to? Luisa lay for a long time brooding over the difficulties and the enormous energy required. Clive would be angry. So would Doctor Lennox and the nurses. She may set her recovery back a long way.

But the vision of Clive with his polished easy friendliness inviting the strange girl cosily into his house—Luisa's house—came to bring the stormy pain to her eyes.

With a new firmness and determination she put out her hand and rang the bell.

IV

Meg looked at her face in the tilted mirror of the train toilet. She wondered again if Derek's words were right. "I don't think it's your secretarial abilities he's interested in. Surely you're not taken in by that."

Derek was speaking with the suspiciousness of a man of the world. Simon Somers, because he came from the same village and knew Clive Wilton, had spoken from more intimate knowledge.

The warnings of both men only served to make Meg more curious as to what awaited her. For by all reports Clive Wilton had a beautiful wife. And he couldn't have shown less interest in Meg's appearance when that funny rather pathetic little artist, Hans Cromer, had grown so enthusiastic about her. He probably liked dark women, not fair ones. Certainly, when he had taken her to lunch, he had looked at her in a penetrating but quite impersonal way. He had been assessing the value of her appearance only so far as his business was concerned. If her wide apart intensely blue eyes and smooth pale hair had little effect on him they would have a decided effect on most men. She would be a decorative asset to his gallery. Also, she had intelligence. Or enough to satisfy him, as he seemed to discover after asking her a series of pertinent questions.

He was completely charming, devoting himself to her with the greatest attention. He said he had been looking for someone like her for a long time, but at the exhibition he had been busy and preoccupied. He had had a sort of doubletake later, remembering her poise and her intelligence.

"I do hope your present position isn't too vital, Miss Burney. You can leave it, can't you, and come to me? You have the appearance, and the secretarial ability, and you're interested in art."

"I didn't tell you I was interested in art," Meg said.

"But you must be. You said you were just back from Florence."

He smiled persuasively, his small dark bright eyes full of warmth and friendliness. He bore no relation to the aloof distrait man she had previously met. He even said that since she spoke Italian it would be nice for his wife to meet her later, when she was a little stronger.

There was utterly nothing to be suspicious about, and Meg's heart leapt at the prospect of a change. She had been so unhappy lately. What she needed to recover from Derek and his charming vagueness and irresponsibility was not just a holiday abroad but a complete change of job and background. Here, like fate, was the opportunity.

And what if it were not, as Derek suggested, her secretarial abilities in which Clive was interested. She could come to no harm in finding out.

But both Derek and Simon must be wrong, for Clive's approach was still quite impersonal. Derek at least was merely suffering from hurt feelings, and serve him right. The reproach in his face had been almost amusing. He was so completely selfish. Perhaps this would teach him not to take her for granted. Or would he promptly forget her?

He had said, "I never thought you'd be so reckless. Anyway, I thought you loved me."

"Heavens, I'm not going to *live* with this man. And it was you who made these rules about no strings."

He would never know what it cost her to speak so lightly. His reproachful gaze gave her both pleasure and pain. Yet once again she knew that he wouldn't suffer too deeply. In a day or two he would be relieved to be entirely free. Was there a shadow of the petulant self-indulgent older man in his face already? Whether he forgot her or not, she must forget him. For this would never have a happy conclusion. She was wise to seize the opportunity to escape, no matter what strange forebodings she had about it.

"Anyway, Clive Wilton's in love with his wife," she added, but not with a great deal of conviction, for Clive had not been persuaded to talk about his wife, the mysterious Luisa.

"She's in the hospital. Will be there for months, I believe."

"What's wrong with her? I didn't like to ask Clive, and he didn't tell me."

"I don't know. Some sort of accident, I believe."

"How tragic for him! That must be why he won't talk about her."

"Don't start feeling too sympathetic for him," Derek said tartly. "The next thing, you'll be in love with him."

"Don't be absurd. I've told you that he only sees me as his secretary."

But did he, and was this tidying up before going to the restaurant car for coffee being done deliberately so that Clive Wilton's lively dark eyes would look on her with more personal interest?

Meg didn't know. She was only determined to shut the thought of Derek out of her mind. That affair was over. In spite of his petulant protests, Derek knew it as well as she did. The farther away from London she got, the better. It didn't much matter where, or in whose company.

Clive was waiting for her in the restaurant car, but he wasn't alone. The young man with the untidy heavy brown hair and the lazy brown eyes that lifted to survey her with cool intentness was with him. Meg's heart skipped a beat, from surprise only. So Simon Somers was there already. She had anticipated meeting him at some time in Frenchley, but not this soon. She didn't know whether she was pleased or resentful about his sudden intrusion, but one thing was clear, Clive was not pleased.

Although Meg knew him slightly, she was already alert to inflections in his voice. Now it had the aloofness it had had in the gallery when Hans Cromer had pushed her forward.

"Meg, this is a neighbor of mine in Frenchley. Simon Somers. Miss Burney, my secretary, Simon."

The young man stood up, smiling at Meg.

"Actually we have met very briefly. At your exhibition, Clive. We even had a bet which I appear to have won."

Meg winced. Clive said politely, "That's interesting. What was the bet?"

"Oh, something about the value of a piece of merchandise. Not one of your pictures, Clive. Well, how nice to meet again, Miss Burney. Frenchley's pretty small and dull. We'll be pleased to have a new face around."

Now what had there been in that perfectly innocent remark to make Clive frown ever so slightly? Or had he frowned? The next moment he said in his smooth easy way, "Some coffee, Meg? Have some coffee with us, Simon? You can tell us what's been going on in Frenchley since I've been in London. How's Janie?"

"Janie's fine. Janie Howard," he explained to Meg, "is our librarian. What she doesn't know about books would fill a book. She's obviously a direct descendant of the Howard who lost her head."

"Janie has a charming head," said Clive, "but Simon's wrong. She won't lose it, she's much too shrewd."

"Let's hope, not in the physical sense, anyway," Simon said lightly. "I wouldn't guarantee any other way."

They both spoke indulgently, but where Clive's voice held deliberate derision, Simon's held affection. Janie was obviously the local character.

"How long are you down for, Clive?" Simon went on.

"I'm not sure. Several weeks, I hope. I've a lot of work that Meg and I will get through at home without disturbances. And of course I want to see my wife as much as possible."

"How is she?"

"Oh, very bright, from her letters. But there's another operation coming up, I'm afraid. It's a slow business. There's no way of hurrying it."

Clive spoke politely, but his face had darkened. Now he abruptly changed the subject.

"How's business, Simon? You had that nice pair of Meissen figures."

"Sold them at Sotheby's for quite a good price. Otherwise business is pretty dull."

"You might have known Frenchley was hardly a thriving center."

"Yes, I know. But I like it."

"Simon has a junk shop," Clive explained to Meg. "Sorry, old man, should I say antique? He scours the countryside."

"I have an eye for a pretty thing," Simon said idly. "Unfortunately, I'm not the only one."

He was indulging in his irritating double talk again. That remark, Meg was sure, had been meant for her. For all his apparent indolence, one felt as if one were under a microscope. She could almost read the thoughts behind those watchful eyes. (Why is Clive Wilton bringing a pretty secretary home while his wife is in the hospital? Why doesn't he leave her in London? Why does she come willingly with a man she scarcely knows? Is she very naïve or simply doesn't give a damn? Or is she doing it from bravado? Or running away from something?)

Whether he in turn read her thought she didn't

know, for he suddenly said with complete unexpect-
edness:

"I've been visiting my mother. She says I should
have a wife. She wants grandchildren. Does every
woman want grandchildren?"

"Children first, I should think," said Clive. He
looked bored. He was wondering how he could
leave. He looked at his empty coffee cup.

Meg took the hint and stood up.

"Are we almost there?"

"In another ten minutes or so. Shall we go and
see to the luggage?"

Simon uncrossed his long legs. "Being met? Like
me to give you a lift?"

"No, thanks, old man. I've arranged for a car."

"How much longer before you can drive?" Simon's
voice was completely casual, but there was no mistaking the tightening of Clive's brows.

"Not long," he said briefly. "Come, Meg."

"Bad luck, old chap. The whole thing was jolly
bad luck."

Simon's cheerful voice followed them with strange
insistence.

"What does he mean?" Meg couldn't help asking
Clive as they went down the corridor. "What was
bad luck?"

"I'd better tell you, since you'll hear soon enough.
When my wife was so badly hurt in an accident, I
was driving. I lost my license for a year."

"Oh, I'm sorry!"

So that explained the dark shadow that came over
his face, his reluctance to talk of his wife's illness.
He was suffering this dreadful guilt for what he
probably imagined had been his own carelessness.

"Thank you, Meg." His grateful voice acknowledged her sincerity. "You won't find everyone in Frenchley so charitable."

"What do you mean?"

He looked away, his face a stern silhouette.

"It's even been suggested the accident was intentional."

"Oh, no! But you were in the car, too!"

"I was somehow thrown clear. Escaped with a broken wrist. My wife had what they call multiple injuries."

Meg touched his arm. His friendliness that had prompted the use of her first name almost at once now permitted her this small familiarity.

"I think you imagine what people say. You torture yourself unnecessarily."

"Do I? I wonder. The thing is, it needn't have happened. I *was* going too fast, and it *was* a wet night. The reflections were bad. I didn't have to hurry so much. But we were late and I was tired, and it's perfectly true, we had had a slight argument. I was tense and irritable—lost my judgment. So it did happen, and it was my fault. But it wasn't intentional."

His vivid slightly monkeyish face was not meant for tragedy. It looked almost comical, and Meg's heart twisted in sympathy.

"How could you think I would believe any of those horrible rumors, Mr. Wilton?"

"Thank you, Meg. Again. But you'll hear the rumors. Simon, you see, has. Perhaps even repeated them."

Meg involuntarily glanced over her shoulder to see if the large young man had followed them down the corridor. She couldn't remember any malice in his observant brown eyes. But it was true that he had made a pointed reference to Clive's being unable to drive the car. As if he had wanted Meg to know the rumors. . . .

Was he trying to warn her about something? Was there really something strange about Clive and his household and his past? Or was Simon just being a little foolish about her welfare?

Was the latter likely—she being a girl Simon had met only twice. Involuntarily Meg smiled. Strangely enough, she didn't find the thought too displeasing.

V

It was getting dark in the studio, but Hans, because he liked to paint by daylight, wouldn't switch on a light. Janie didn't like the dark at any time, she was one for bright lights and plenty of noise and laughter. Apart from finding the gloom depressing, in this house it was even a little eerie.

She wriggled and asked petulantly, "How much longer do I have to sit here?"

"Just a little longer, please."

"Oh, Hans! And you won't even let me see what you've done. You make me dress up in this tight thing and suffer. I'd have you know I'm slowly dying. I can't breathe. I have a twenty-four waist, I might say.

"And very nice, too."

"Yes, but this is a twenty-two, if not a twenty."

"I'm sorry, darling. It was the only one I had. And too tight or not, you look quite perfect in it."

Janie, on her perch in the cool ramshackle studio, sighed again. If Hans wasn't so sweet she wouldn't sit here a minute longer. She'd been here for hours and her back was breaking. But she was crazy about him, with his funny worried face, those big melting eyes, and his caressing way of talking in that deep foreign voice. She had never known anyone like him before. She really thought she might be in love with him. It was a pity he was so poor, living in this freezing half-furnished house without an atom of comfort, and it didn't seem likely he would ever be less poor. Messing around as he did with painting when he wasn't a good artist and never would be. Everyone said so, even Clive Wilton, although Clive was decent enough to try to sell his pictures.

She only sat for him because she liked him so much, and he said those wonderful things to her.

"Your face is unique, Janie darling. Oh sure, I know I am a bad artist, but I have this longing all the time to capture beautiful faces, and preserve them forever. Perhaps what I do of you will be a masterpiece, no?"

"What's so unique about my face?" Janie had always been dissatisfied with the way she looked, her pale oval face with its small pouting mouth and prominent dark eyes had seemed uninteresting, almost plain. And her hair was quite straight. She had had it curled and fluffed up until Hans had begged her to brush it quite smooth and draw it back over her ears. That had made her look more old-fashioned than ever, but he had gone into raptures.

"Exquisite. You are now the period of your ancestor."

"My ancestor?"

"The lady who loved the wicked king and lost her head."

Janie looked puzzled, but not displeased.

"She's not my ancestor and I promise you I won't fall in love with anyone as dangerous as old Henry."

"But you like danger a little? It brightens your eyes."

What an odd thing to say. Yet it was true, her heart did quicken. And she adored compliments. She was ready to put on the strange old-fashioned clothes, a tightly waisted dress with billowing sleeves in dull red brocade, and thread pearls (Woolworth's) through her hair, and sit here for hours just to hear Hans saying those silly exciting things to her. He was a bit daft, really. Working away for hours when the only thing he could really paint were landscapes. And those not very well apparently, although she thought they were pretty. Anyway, he was very poor and couldn't afford to get decent furniture or repair the house, which was falling to bits. And the only help he had was that of the eccentric elderly Miss Burt who didn't particularly want money so long as she had a room for herself and her cat.

Miss Burt's housework and cooking were sketchy, to say the least. She had an obsession that one day she would go blind, and therefore liked all the rooms as dark as possible to save eye strain, and never went out when the sun was shining. No one but kind uncritical Hans would bother with her.

He said, "Poor old soul, let her be. She suits me very well. If she likes some days to stay in her room, then I manage."

This arrangement suited Janie too, because it

meant Miss Burt didn't come prying, and if Hans wanted to kiss her a bit when he stopped work there was no fear of interruption.

Janie wriggled again and said, "Oh, darling, do let me get down. I'm going to faint."

"Just one little moment. What's the time?"

"It's nearly five o'clock. I've got to get back to open the library."

Hans threw down his brush. "Then I must stop, because the train will be in."

"The train? Who's coming?"

"Clive and his new secretary."

"You never told me he was getting a new secretary. What's happened to his old one?"

"Oh, she was no good. No personality, no looks."

Janie raised her eyebrows. "Couldn't even type, I suppose. Can this new one? Or did he forget to ask her? And why is he bringing her home with him?"

"To do his work, of course."

"He never brought his last one home."

"He intends to work more at home, as far as I know. To be nearer his wife. And anyway his other secretary wouldn't have fitted into his home."

"Then he is starting an affair with her! While his wife's in the hospital."

"Oh, no, not an affair like that. Just an affair of work."

Hans, of course, was so naïve. Or pretended to be. For now his square dark face held a different look. Of excitement? Anticipation?

"Have you seen this girl?" Janie demanded jealously. "Is she pretty?"

"Yes, I've seen her. She's pretty. Blonde, blue eyes. Looks very innocent, though she may not be that innocent."

"I'll bet she's not. What's her name"

"Margaret Burney. Meg. Why, what is it, my darling? You look cross. Are you jealous of Clive and his pretty secretary?"

"It wasn't Clive who was looking at the time the train came in. It was you."

Hans looked guilty and repentant. "I'm sorry. You're right. I always get like this about a new face. You know that. It doesn't mean anything except that I want to get it on canvas. And I'm so bad. I try so hard. You should be sorry for me, little Janie, not cross with me. What do I care for this girl's pink and white face otherwise? It leaves me cold. I like dark hair, dark eyes. Come here, my little one."

"Hey, wait a minute!" said Janie. "I want to get out of this dress first. Otherwise you might be imagining yourself Henry the Eighth."

He had come close to her.

"So I might." His fingers caressed her throat playfully.

"Put up that screen," ordered Janie. "And wait till I change."

Her voice was calm enough, but inwardly she was beginning to tremble. It was partly from excitement, partly from fear. Hans had this effect on her, and she found it irresistible. In comparison, all other men seemed dull. She was drawn back to this quiet dark house even when she had a queer unexplainable apprehension about it.

While she was unlacing the heavy brocade dress the telephone rang. Even that seemed oddly significant, for Hans left the room abruptly, without apology, as if he had been waiting for the call. He was downstairs for some time, and Janie, dressed now in her loose sweater and skirt, prowled about restlessly.

She took a quick forbidden look at the sketch Hans had been making of her. It looked queer and old-fashioned. Her eyes protruded and her nose looked too thin. Surely she didn't really look like that. Hans certainly was a bad painter, poor darling. No wonder he kept telling her she wasn't to look at what he was doing. What else had he got tucked away in this moldy old place? Plenty of things that no one would buy. How on earth did he live?

Janie fingered the dusty canvas turned to the wall. She had never been left alone in this room before. Now was her opportunity to look around. She pulled some curtains aside inquisitively, and found that they hid not a window but a door. Did it lead into a cupboard, or another attic room? She turned the knob, but the door was locked, or jammed tight with damp and age.

"What are you doing?"

Hans' voice, loud and sudden, made her spin around. It was getting dark, and for a moment, while she couldn't see his face clearly, it looked dark and sinister, and queerly threatening.

Her breath caught.

"I'm not doing anything. I just wondered where this door went."

"It goes down some steps all the way to the cellar. If you're a naughty girl I may push you down them."

"Hans!" She was half shocked, half thrilled.

But he was smiling. "I found this old house full of surprises. Unpleasant ones. Damp, woodworm, steps to break your neck. I keep that door locked just so it won't break anyone's neck. Now come, little one. I want to kiss you."

Janie went willingly. He wasn't very young. He

must be forty at least. She usually fell in love with much younger men. Even Simon Somers, who had remained annoyingly impervious to her approaches, was younger. But there was something about Hans, the way he kissed, his urgency, the excitement of his touch. It was all mixed up with wearing the medieval dress and listening to the strange enthralling things he said about her. She didn't think she would be able to hold him off much longer.

"Who was that ringing you?"

"Clive."

"Has he got the girl?"

"Has he brought home his new secretary, you mean?"

"I don't think it's very nice of him with his wife still in the hospital," Janie said righteously. "I suppose you can't wait to see this girl."

"I'm going there to dinner tonight."

Janie drew back. "There you are, you can't wait to see her!"

"I'm seeing Clive because at last he has sold a picture for me. And for a good price. We have to celebrate."

"Congratulations!" said Janie glumly.

"And if the little blonde is at dinner I will look at her as an artist would. Not the way I'm looking at you now. Janie, Janie, why do you have such an exciting face? I can't get it out of my mind."

Janie relaxed. This was better. She believed he meant it. But why, oh why did she have to lose her head over a penniless artist? She was nuts.

She went home a little later, calling good-bye loudly to Miss Burt who didn't answer.

She had a room in the Crown overlooking the narrow High Street. Opposite it was Simon Somer's antique shop. She noticed that Simon's light was on upstairs, and threw up her window to lean out.

"Hi, Simon! Have a good time visiting your mother?"

Simon's window opened in response.

"Fine, thank you, Janie. How's the reading public?"

"Awful. I'm fed up with their silly tastes. Even the vicar's taken to who-dun-its."

"Where have you been, Janie? You've got paint on your face."

"Oh, that's Hans. I've been giving him a sitting."

She could just see Simon's face in the dusk, his hair falling untidily.

"Are you sure it's only painting Hans is interested in?"

His voice was lazy, as usual, but it provoked Janie. Where would girls be if all men were like Simon Somers, merely, it seemed, amused and slightly cynical observers of life? And full of warnings, like maiden aunts. Besides, Simon knew nothing about Hans. He was judging him without a hearing.

"If Hans thinks he can be a successful portrait painter, why shouldn't he try," she said indignantly. "After all, you're trying to be a success at your job."

"So I am."

"Well, don't say it as if you expect to get there when you know Hans won't."

"I'm not at all sure Hans won't. Wherever it is he's planning to get, of course."

Janie shrugged. "Well, I know Hans has this obsession about painting, poor darling. I'm never really sure whether he wants to paint pretty faces, or kiss

44

them. He's a little mixed up. But it's only kind to humor him, to a certain extent, that is," Janie added judiciously. "He's had a ghastly time in Holland with all those Germans around. He might have been a great painter if he'd had a chance when he was young. Anyway, he's sold a picture. He's heard from Clive Wilton who's just home."

"I know. I came down on the train with them."

Janie leaned out eagerly. "With the new secretary? What's she like? As pretty as Hans said?"

"Janie, my poppet, I don't have the standards of an aspiring portrait painter."

"But you do have feelings, don't you? Are you going to fall for her, too?"

"Too?"

"Well, Clive must have. Or why did he bring her here? Why did she come?"

"Perhaps, because she really thinks it's a good job. And perhaps it is. Why shouldn't it be?"

"With the face of an angel?" Janie said skeptically. "I didn't think that was a particular requirement of a secretary."

"And you, Janie Howard," said Simon with some asperity, "have the face of a sixteenth century slut."

VI

Mrs. Coombe, Clive's housekeeper, had been telephoned to expect Clive and his new secretary. She had dutifully prepared one of the spare rooms for Meg, and took her to it politely enough, but obviously with the greatest disapproval.

She was a lean harsh-looking woman who looked as if she never smiled, and it was very difficult to imagine what the late Mr. Coombe had looked like. Perhaps he had died in self-defense. Clive had explained that he had a highly-respectable housekeeper who was a widow. He had told Meg not to be alarmed by her, she was somewhat distant, but she was a most capable woman, and devoted to his wife.

"Luisa calls her Lena," he said. "I confess I scarcely have the courage."

There was one thought uppermost in Meg's mind when she had come into the house, and that was to see a photograph of Luisa. There must be several about, if not indeed a portrait. Clive would not have married a woman who was not eminently paintable. She knew him well enough already to know that. And she could not get rid of the lurking suspicion that Luisa was really Angelica, but that for some reason Clive had wished to keep that a secret. Probably he preferred Angelica's pathetically poor and tragic childhood to be forgotten. He would not want it known that he had married a Cinderella.

"How is Mrs. Wilton?" Meg asked the forbidding Lena, who had shown her into a bedroom that seemed to be the farthest possible from the main rooms in the house.

"She is improving, thank you, miss."

Meg, despite the woman's obvious unwillingness to answer questions, was determined to go on.

"Is she well enough to have visitors yet? I mean strangers. I'd like so much to go and see her."

"I expect you'll see her soon enough. Will you use the guest bathroom, miss? I've put towels in there. It's the second door on the right."

Lena was preparing to go. She hadn't really answered anything.

"I didn't like to ask Mr. Wilton—but are his wife's injuries very bad?"

"As bad as—anyone—could wish."

The woman really was going now. Her answer had told Meg nothing and yet, in another way, everything. There had been such deliberation about the use of that word "anyone." She had meant Clive, of course. Or did she, as her cold hostile eyes flicked over Meg's slim figure, mean Meg herself?

For all her determination to like this job and her new surroundings, Meg felt slightly chilled. Surely this nasty suspicious woman didn't imagine she had come here to attempt to take Luisa's place?

But it was perfectly true that Clive had not had a secretary in his home before. He had told her that. But he had also explained that he had an enormous accumulation of work, and if he remained in London to do it he couldn't visit his wife every day, which he wanted to do. He hadn't deceived her in any way. And although he had been perfectly charming to her ever since their first lunch together, his behavior had never been in the least intimate.

Oh well, no doubt there would be gossip. This must be a gossipy kind of place, with those horrid things being said about Clive already. She must do her best to dispel suspicion. And she really wanted to be a friend of Luisa's—or Angelica's. The poor girl, so badly injured that no one told her exactly what her injuries were, must need all the friends she could get.

Meg unpacked in the small but charming bedroom whose window looked out over a field, with the roofs of the village beyond that, then took a leisurely bath in the blue and white guest bathroom, and dressed for dinner.

Clive had told her he was asking Hans Cromer over. Hans would want to meet her again, since he had so admired her, and anyway they had a small celebration since he had been lucky enough to sell one of Hans' water colors.

"Don't be too embarrassed if Hans admires you too extravagantly," he said. "He gets like that about attractive women. He only has this desire to put their faces on canvas, but unfortunately his desire is a great deal bigger than his talent."

"Will he want to paint me?" Meg asked.

"Quite likely. But don't let him make a nuisance of himself. I think we're all inclined to humor him because of his tragic past. He went through the occupation, and was the only survivor of his family. It makes a deep mark on a man."

"You're very kind to him, Mr. Wilton."

"Oh, no. No more than to anyone else."

Clive certainly did seem open and kind and honest, and she didn't want to misjudge him. But there still did linger in her memory that overheard conversation when Hans had been begging Clive to do something, assuring him that the risk was negligible. It couldn't have been anything to do with her, could it? And yet the very next day he had rung her, startling her by his invitation to lunch.

Oh well, something intriguing and slightly mysterious like this was what she had wanted to take her mind off Derek. Already Derek seemed very far away, although her heart still ached stubbornly. Fleetingly, the thought crossed her mind that Simon Somers might prove a more effective way of curing heartache than any of Clive's or Hans' intrigues. Simply because Simon refused to be ignored, nothing else.

Now she was ready for dinner, and if the fearsome Lena was occupied in the kitchen, as she ought to be, there would be an opportunity to stroll through the downstairs rooms, looking casually for photographs.

There were none, however, in the drawing-room. It was a rather severely furnished room, that did not look lived in. Meg wondered fleetingly if Luisa liked the modern painting over the fireplace with its brilliant harsh colors, or the stark lines of the comfortable but uninviting furniture. The colors were fresh and vivid and curiously hypnotic. But there was nothing feminine about the room. It all suggested Clive's influence, or probably his entire choice. And it was not a room for sentimental family photographs. She must look elsewhere for those.

She wondered how she could get into Luisa's bedroom. If she made quite sure Lena was in the kitchen, and Clive downstairs. . . .

As the thought crossed her mind she heard Clive speaking on the telephone in his study across the hall. And the sound of dishes indicated that Lena was in the kitchen.

It took only a moment to slip back upstairs, and walk along the passage, deciding which was the main bedroom. It would overlook the front garden. It must be this one.

Meg took a deep breath and opened the door.

There was a double bed with a heavy satin quilt, a deep luxurious carpet, and a white and gilt dressing table. Clive's suitcase stood open on the floor.

There was a photograph on the table beside the bed. Meg went swiftly to look at it. But to her disappointment it was one of Clive. He was unsmiling and looked distinguished, more handsome than he really was. The photographer had flattered him. He had also caught a certain ruthlessness. Or was it just a look of keen ambition?

Meg looked about disappointedly. There was no other photograph in the room. If Clive had one of his wife he had it somewhere else.

A little ashamed of her inquisitiveness, Meg tiptoed out of the room and went downstairs again. After all, if she had by some extraordinary chance discovered that Luisa really was Angelica, what was she to do or say? It was no business of hers.

Nevertheless, the thought nagged at her. Clive came into the drawing-room presently, and suggested cocktails.

"What are you going to drink? Can I mix you a martini?"

"I'd love it. This is a charming room."

"Do you like it? I've a passion for uncluttered rooms, and I'm all for present-day designers. Give them a chance. After all, where would William Morris or Chippendale have been if they hadn't been given a chance by their contemporaries. Most women, of course, don't like this starkness."

"Does your wife?" Meg asked casually.

Clive looked tolerant.

"Oh, Luisa's very young. She simply left everything to me. We couldn't have classical Italy in an English village, so she preferred to trust my judgment."

Angelica was young, too, Meg thought fleetingly.

"Is your wife beautiful? Have you a picture of her?"

Clive was shaking the cocktail shaker with con-centration.

"Not here, no. I have some in London. Here, I have Luisa herself. Now, will you taste this and tell me if it's to your liking."

She took the glass obediently, and sipped the drink. She realized that he had evaded her ques-tions, and she had learnt exactly nothing.

Hans arrived a few minutes later. Meg heard him talking to Clive in the hall.

"It's nice to have you back, Clive. Did you have a good journey?"

"Fine, thanks."

"And Luisa? Is the news good?"

"As good as can be expected."

Meg had a curious idea that this polite ordinary conversation was meant for her ears, for a moment later Hans lowered his voice and said something rapidly.

Clive answered briefly. "You'll have to judge for yourself." And Hans, speaking audibly again, said, "It's all right. I couldn't have made a mistake. I know."

As they came near the door, Clive said clearly, again for Meg's benefit: "Wasn't that splendid about the sale of your picture. A stockbroker's wife from Surrey bought it, bless her. Come and see if you remember my new secretary. You ought to, since you admired her enough at the show."

The two men came in and Hans greeted Meg. He held her hand a moment longer than necessary.

"How nice to see you here, Miss Burney. I credit myself with discovering you for Clive."

"Thank you, old chap. The debt's acknowledged,"

Clive said easily, and changed the subject to a discussion of his exhibition. But although Hans listened intelligently enough, he never took his eyes off Meg.

She became uneasy and embarrassed by his intense regard. Didn't Clive notice how he stared at her? The odd thing was that his regard did not seem so much admiring as calculating. As if he were wondering whether she would stand up to some test. In London she had thought him harmless and rather pathetic, with his large admiring brown eyes and air of resigned failure. But now there was no hint of failure about him. He had a look of triumph.

Lena waited on the table with gloomy efficiency. From an expression Meg caught on her face, Meg fancied that she, too, did not care for Hans. But then she didn't seem madly enthusiastic about anybody except her mistress.

Probably she resented other people being well and enjoying her well-cooked food while Luisa was so ill.

The drinks and the food, instead of making Meg feel relaxed and content, produced in her a state of haziness and depression and anxiety—or was that state caused by her two companions. What had she got herself into? The two men, Hans openly staring, Clive more subtle but also observant of her every gesture, made her think idiotically of two large male cats watching one defenseless mouse. . . . One began to wonder, even more senselessly, whether Luisa, too, had been a mouse. . . .

"Let's have coffee in the other room," Clive was saying. "Meg, I won't ask you to have more wine because I want to do a little work later on."

"Tonight? You'll make her work tonight?" Hans said.

"Is that being unfair, Meg? I like to work at night. It's the reason I want a resident secretary."

The telephone began to ring across the hall.

Clive shrugged. "There you are, you see. The moment I'm home."

"Shall I answer it, Mr. Wilton?" Meg asked.

"If you would. Lena, we'll have coffee in the drawing-room."

Meg hurried into the cool study to answer the patiently br-rr-ing telephone.

A brisk voice said in her ear, "Is that Mr. Wilton's house? Can I speak to Mr. Wilton, please?"

"Who is it speaking?"

"It's the hospital at Rye. The head nurse would like to speak to Mr. Wilton."

Meg put down the receiver and hastened with the message. Clive looked startled. So did Hans. Meg caught a flashed glance between them.

"Is it bad news?" Hans asked.

Clive said tensely, "I hope not," and went out.

For the first time Hans looked at Meg without that embarrassing intensity. He was now apparently concerned and alarmed for Clive.

"Will it be some trouble?" said Meg. "Mr. Wilton seemed alarmed."

"But of course he would. It's his wife. He's had so much worry. If Luisa has had a relapse he'll be in agony. He is so sensitive. He suffers with her."

"Were her injuries so bad?" Meg asked.

"Oh, quite serious, yes. But it's now more the effect of the shock. On her mind, you understand."

"Oh! Is that why—" She stopped speaking as understanding came. If Luisa were mentally affected, no wonder Clive evaded questions about her. It must be so distressing. "Mr. Wilton blames himself," she added.

Hans nodded. "But it was simply an accident. It could have happened to anybody. And she was so beautiful, too! No wonder Clive is in despair."

Hans had said that before, in the same melancholy voice. But of course he was obsessed with women's beauty. He would think the loss of that more tragic than the loss of sanity.

Clive came back, walking briskly.

"It's all right," he said. "No alarm. Luisa just knew I would be home this evening. She wanted to send a message."

"Oh, splendid, Clive. I'm so glad. How is she?"

"The nurse says she's better, actually. Some brandy, Hans? Meg?"

Only someone who knew Clive well, or someone as inquisitive and observant as she, Meg thought, would have noticed the tension beneath his calm voice. He had lit a cigarette and was puffing it quickly. His hand was slightly clenched.

And, why, if it was so easy to get in touch with the hospital, did Luisa have to call? Why hadn't he called her?

"No brandy for me, thank you, Mr. Wilton, since we're to work," Meg said.

"Yes, so we were." Clive was busy at the sideboard. He didn't turn to look at her. "But I believe I've changed my mind. I'm a little tired. You are, too, I can see."

"And I must go home and put the cat out," Hans said. "I have a housekeeper who is very nervous," he explained to Meg. "She is afraid to open the door

54

after ten o'clock at night. And she is afraid to go out in the daytime if the sun is shining in case it blinds her. Yes, really! She has an obsession about it. She is an eccentric. But she does very well for me, a poor painter."

"Don't believe him, Meg," Clive said over his shoulder. "He's a benefactor to poor old Miss Burt. No one else would have her."

Hans flung out his hands deprecatingly. "Well, she simply lives in one of my rooms. With her cat. On most days she remembers to clean and cook. If she doesn't, I do it myself. She is no bother, poor old soul. And I couldn't afford your efficient Lena, Clive. She alarms me. I confess I'd rather have my silly Miss Burt, who talks to almost no one but her cat. I am so glad Luisa is growing better." He had stood up to go. "Thank you for an excellent dinner, Clive. And one day I hope you will spare Miss Burney for a few hours."

Meg looked up in surprise. Clive smiled.

"Hans simply wants to paint you, Meg."

"I am doing little Janie Howard from the library. She has a most exciting Elizabethan face. But Miss Burney here is Italian renaissance. She has such calm and purity. Please don't think me crazy, Miss Burney. My portraits are abominable. But still I must try. One day it will come, I tell myself."

"I'm sure Meg won't mind giving you a little time one day," Clive said.

"No," Meg echoed automatically. She didn't understand what was going on. If Hans' portraits were so bad, why did Clive encourage him? However, if she went she would see Hans' studio and the mad Miss Burt with her cat. And perhaps dark Janie Howard. It was all exciting and different, and the best thing that could have happened to her. She was prepared to agree to almost everything.

When Hans had gone, Clive said, "Go to bed, Meg. We'll make an early start in the morning. And sleep well. Don't be alarmed if you hear noises in the night. I sometimes walk about, and so does Lena."

"Yes, Mr. Wilton." He was still preoccupied and looked tired and pale. Meg supposed he was thinking of his wife, and she added, "I'm so glad your wife is better. I hope I'll be able to see her later on."

"But of course. It will do her good. She needs young friends. We're all going to get along very well, I'm sure."

Now he seemed to be reassuring her. Or was that her imagination? For he was restless and tense, impatient for her to go upstairs and leave him.

"Close your door, Meg, so we won't disturb you."

"Yes, Mr. Wilton. Good night."

Upstairs, Meg undressed slowly, throwing her clothes on a chair, her earrings and gold bangle on the dressing table.

She was tired enough to sleep. But everything was now so strange and perplexing that sleep didn't seem likely. Sometime after she had gone to bed she heard a car stop and a door slam. But her window faced the back of the house so she couldn't see whether the car had stopped at this house or not. In any case, it was none of her business. Quelling her impulse to open her door and listen, she turned over and resolutely determined to sleep.

She almost succeeded. It was half in a dream that she heard voices raised—or was it owls calling—and later still that she thought she heard the click of the lock of her own door.

This brought her sharply awake. But she must have imagined that, too, for moonlight coming in the room showed the door closed. A rising wind was swishing in the curtains—or was it a rustling outside the door that she could hear?

The door handle *was* turning!

Meg scarcely breathed as the door opened. She wanted to call out, "Who is it?" but ridiculously she had lost her voice. She lay petrified, watching a shadowy form appear.

A man? A woman?

There seemed to be no face, just an indistinguishable paleness.

A head like an egg, smooth and white.

At last Meg did give a strangled scream. There was a little gasp from the doorway, and then a slightly muffled voice:

"I'm so sorry. I didn't mean to wake you."

The voice was light and breathless, a woman's voice.

Meg struggled up. "Who are you? What do you want?"

The form was disappearing into the shadows of the doorway. Meg started out of bed, impelled by a strange urgency. This person must not be allowed to disappear.

"Don't go! Tell me what you're looking for. Can I help you?"

"No, not at all."

Light dawned on Meg. "You're Luisa, aren't you?" she said eagerly.

"How do you know?"

"Who else could you be? But I thought you were very ill in the hospital."

The girl answered reluctantly, rather sullenly. "I came home this evening. My husband says I shouldn't have. He was—upset. But I was well enough. I simply told the nurse I was leaving."

"If you're well enough to walk about like this, then I should think you are well enough to be home," Meg said practically. "I'm sure your husband really is pleased."

She was trying to prolong the conversation, not wanting the stranger to go.

"Yes? You think so?" The voice was skeptical, yet pathetically eager.

"But didn't you know I was here?" Meg went on. "Did you think this room was empty? If there's something you're looking for, do take it."

There was a little silence. Then the girl said deliberately out of the darkness, "I knew you were here. I came to see you."

The animosity in her voice made Meg hesitate. What had the poor thing been told? Was she jealous? She said practically, "Well, we can't see each other in the dark. Wait till I find the light. I want to see you, too, because I believe—"

The girl cut off Meg's words. "No, don't! Don't put on the light!"

There was panic in her voice. She had moved quickly to the bedside, and held her hand over the light switch, barring Meg. Meg could see only the white strangely blank blur of her face.

"But why not?" she asked perplexedly.

"Because you will get a shock."

The voice, speaking deliberate almost perfect

English, did have a faintly familiar sound. Meg recognized it with excitement.

"I believe you *are* Angelica. Your husband says you're not, but I remember your voice."

There was the briefest pause. Then, "Who is Angelica?" came the cool voice.

Meg was momentarily baffled. She had been so sure her intuition was right.

"I thought you were. I'm Meg Burney. Don't you remember me coming to your villa in Florence? I talked to you and your grandmother. I apologize if I'm making a mistake, but your voice is awfully similar. Do let me see you!"

"No, no!"

Meg had another intuition.

"I won't tell your husband if you don't want him to know. Is that why he said you weren't Angelica? Because you never told him? Didn't you want him to know how poor you were, and the house falling down."

"The house—falling down. . . ."

"I don't suppose you knew about that. You'd left it before the storm, hadn't you?"

The dim figure stood quite still. She said nothing now, making no sign whether or not she knew what Meg was talking about.

Meg moved impatiently.

"You said you wanted to see me. You can't without some light."

"Are you—very pretty?"

The girl sounded apprehensive, frightened, not much more than a child. How could someone as sophisticated as Clive Wilton have married this uncertain young creature?

Meg said disappointedly, "If you're Angelica, you'd remember what I looked like. No, I'm not that pretty. Only Hans thinks so."

"*Hans!*"

Luisa had stiffened. Meg couldn't decide whether her voice had held surprise or terror.

"Has he been here already? He doesn't waste much time, does he?"

"Why do you say that?"

"I don't know. I don't know. My husband says I'm neurotic, I have strange fancies. Or dreams. I don't know which. But what has happened—is no dream. Look at me! Put on the light and look at me! You had better, after all."

Meg fumbled for the light switch. The girl's disturbed state of mind had communicated itself to her. Her fingers trembled.

The light flooding the room showed the cylindrically bandaged head, the slits for eyes, for nose, for mouth. Nothing else. No hair, no features. . . .

"Oh!" whispered Meg. "You poor thing."

Then Clive's voice, harsh and angry, came from the doorway.

"Luisa, what are you doing here? Didn't I tell you to stay in your room?"

VII

The little figure of Luisa shrank against the dressing table. Clive bent all his anger on her, ignoring Meg's presence.

"Where's Lena? Hasn't she got your bed ready? You should be there after your journey. What's the doctor going to say? First of all running away from the hospital, and now staying up to all hours. Don't you want to get well?"

It was impossible to see whether Luisa was crying. She hung her head docilely, and said in her careful English, "I just wanted to see your new secretary. You wrote to me about her. I wanted to be home when she was here."

"You could have met Meg in the morning. You didn't need to frighten her tonight."

"Frighten?" The uncertain voice faltered.

Meg was dragging on her dressing gown.

"She didn't do that, Mr. Wilton. She merely came to talk to me."

"She's too impulsive. Aren't you, my sweet? You could have waited until the morning. Coming home was enough for one day. Quite apart from disturbing Miss Burney's rest."

Meg watched Clive put his arm round the drooping figure. Oh, be kind to her, be kind to her! she was begging him silently.

But Luisa had gathered her self-possession and dignity.

"I'm perfectly all right, Clive. I'm so much better. The doctor said a little time at home before the next operation would be good for me."

"Then, my darling, you should have told me and I would have come for you."

"I wanted—to surprise you."

Clive looked at her with a long thoughtful look. Meg wished she could read what was behind his now gentle and calm face. Was he thinking that

61

Luisa had deliberately chosen to come late and un-announced to see what Clive might be doing with his new secretary?

"You're not angry, are you? I only wanted to be with you."

Uncertainty had come back into Luisa's voice. Clive said tenderly, "Angry! My darling, I'm delighted you're well enough to be home. It's only that I should have brought you. Coming in a hired car like that, and so late. Never mind, you must come straight to bed and rest."

Watching them go, Luisa leaning against Clive's taller figure, they seemed to be all affection.

But a moment ago Clive had been angry. His face had been as hard as stone. And Luisa was nervous, almost frightened. . . .

Why hadn't he said earlier that Luisa was coming home? He had known because the nurse at the hospital had telephoned. Why hadn't he come back into the room and told Meg and Hans the news, instead of keeping it to himself? Hadn't he wanted to disturb Meg late at night? Or shock her with the news that his beautiful young wife had severe facial injuries involving a series of operations? Or could it be that he had wanted to keep Luisa out of Meg's sight, removing her quickly early in the morning and never admitting that she had been home?

That last thought was the most disturbing of all. Meg couldn't go back to bed. She was still sitting on the side of it when Clive came back.

He knocked and came in at her request.

"I'm sorry about that, Meg. You must have been frightened. I didn't want you to see Luisa until the morning. It's always a shock to everybody."

"Is she badly disfigured?"

"She was, but it's coming right. She's extremely sensitive about it, of course, and doesn't want to be seen with the bandages off. But the surgeon promises her a new face, almost as beautiful."

"It's tragic."

"I know. I know."

Clive seemed so distressed that Meg forgot her suspicions.

"Now I understand why you didn't want to talk about her."

"Yes. And I must warn you she's still suffering from shock. She's inclined to say odd things. Did she talk strangely to you?"

"No. She just wanted to see me, she said."

"Oh, yes. I'd written and told her about you. She was very interested. She's lonely, poor child. She hadn't been in England long enough to make friends before this happened. You'll be kind to her, Meg?"

"Of course."

"Thank you, my dear. You're very understanding. Talk to her about Rome. She's still a little homesick."

"Does she have to go back to the hospital right away?" Meg asked.

"I'll talk to the doctor tomorrow. Apparently he thinks a little time at home will do her good. But if we keep her here, have patience with her, Meg. She's inclined, as I said, to imagine things."

The bangle glinted on the table beside the bed. It was the first thing Luisa saw when she opened her eyes in the morning.

She started up eagerly, and was slipping it on to her wrist when Clive came in from the bathroom, tying his tie.

"Clive, is it for me?"

"No, my darling. I just left it there for you to see."

"But why—" Luisa's voice faltered uncertainly. "Whose is it, if it isn't mine?"

"Are you sure you don't know?"

"Of course I don't, Clive. I've never seen it before."

"It's Miss Burney's. Meg's."

"Meg's! Then why is it here?"

"Hadn't you better ask yourself that?"

"But I didn't take it, Clive. Truly!" Luisa's voice was panic-stricken. "I only went to Meg's room last night to see what she looked like. You had said— she was pretty." Her voice faltered again.

"Nevertheless it was in the pocket of your dressing gown."

"But I don't remember—I couldn't have—"

"You never do remember. Do you, darling?" Clive was looking down at her. His face was tired, but quite kind and understanding. "That's one of the difficulties."

Luisa was overcome with horror and doubt.

"I wanted to ask you to buy a gold bracelet for that nice new nurse. But not one like this. I wanted a charm one. So I couldn't have been thinking of that. . . ." Her voice died away uncertainly. She so loved the pretty things she had never had, the earrings and necklaces behind thick glass in jewelers' windows, sometimes left lying on bureaus in homes they visited. She knew their fatal attraction for her. . . .

"Clive—don't tell Miss Burney—"

"If I make that promise, you must make one, too."

He was still looking at her kindly, sympathetically, as if he genuinely loved her and wanted to protect her.

She nodded eagerly. "I promise. And I know what it is that you're going to ask me. No telling secrets."

"You've never seen Meg before?"

He seemed to be asking her a question, but she knew that he was testing her.

"Where would I have seen her before? I've only been in England two years, and six months of that time in the hospital."

"Not in Italy?"

"But of course not, Clive."

Clive patted her hand. "I'll slip the bracelet back into her room sometime. If she's missed it, we'll say Lena moved it, dusting. Don't worry, darling. And I promise you one for the nice nurse."

"Oh, Clive—"

"Then don't cry. And listen, darling, there's no need for all these bandages now. You know there isn't. They should be left off. You haven't even put them on properly."

Luisa shrank back. "But I look like someone else. You don't like me like this."

"Darling, you have only a few scars now, not even particularly noticeable. After the next operation even they won't show. And inside you're exactly the same. You're the girl I fell in love with. So don't be foolish. No more running away, no taking jewelry that I can easily buy for you, no romancing about things that have never happened. . . ."

The light voice held a threat. Luisa nodded eagerly. Already she was determined to be happier. Clive must love her or he wouldn't be so gentle, so understanding.

"Don't make it harder for me," Clive was going

on. "It was all my fault, I know. I have to live with that knowledge."

"It was an accident," Luisa protested.

"An avoidable one. Even I realize that now that it's too late. Well, then?" He raised his brows whimsically. "You'll be good? Nice to Meg. No tricks."

"She really is your secretary?"

"Good heavens, yes. What did you think she was?"

"I don't know, really."

Clive looked at her concernedly.

"What are you afraid of, Luisa? Surely you didn't think I brought Meg here because I was personally interested in her. Apart from anything else, you know I don't care for blondes."

"Then is she such a good secretary?"

"She's the type I want."

"Is Hans going to paint her?"

"Probably. He's already mad about her coloring. You know what he is. Poor old Hans."

"Don't let him, Clive."

"Don't let him!" Clive was mildly astonished. "What Hans does is none of my business, and what Meg does in her spare time is nothing to do with me, either. Anyway, he's wrapped up in Janie Howard at present. Gracious, Luisa, you don't take Hans seriously?"

"I just don't know why you bother with him," Luisa murmured. "He isn't a good artist. You know that. And somehow—he frightens me."

"Oh, darling! That's your imagaination again. Now I'm going to tell Lena to bring your breakfast. And if you really behave and get these silly ideas out of your head I promise you can stay home for a little while."

She was transparently delighted. "Oh, can I? You said last night I couldn't, that I must go back at once."

"Last night I was annoyed with your foolishness. But today's another day. Now I must go and work. Meg and I have a busy morning. I'll send her to you to say good morning, just to give me an opportunity to replace this bracelet. But don't keep her. Remember, she's here to work."

When he had gone out Luisa very slowly began unwinding the clumsy bandage. It was true that without it she had felt too naked to come home, and the nice nurse, Miss Green, had humored her and put it on lightly, telling her she must take it off as soon as she had arrived.

"You must get used to people seeing you, Mrs. Wilton. You'll never get well until then. And really, you don't look bad at all."

Alone in the safety of her room, Luisa picked up a mirror and looked at her face.

Actually, as the nurse had said, it wasn't too bad now. The first operation had repaired her chin and nose, although they didn't look quite like her own any longer, and the next one would take care of the long puckered scar across her left cheek.

One of her eyes now looked slightly bigger than the other through the dragging of the skin, so that she looked like a stranger. And her hair had only just begun to grow again, being short and wispy instead of the smooth dark mass it had been.

She would never be beautiful again, she thought. She would have to look at other unmarked women,

women like Meg, smooth and fair and glowing, and wonder why this had happened to her and not to them. For the rest of her life. She would begin to hate them. She would see the inevitable admiration in men's eyes and know it was always for others, for people like Janie Howard and Meg. Just as she had once envied other girls their pretty clothes and jewelry, now she was going to envy them their unmarked faces. She couldn't yield to that overwhelming temptation and steal a pretty face, but she could think of things like sorrow and old age and illness seizing them. Or even accidents.

A sly look came into Luisa's eyes. Her mouth pinched together. She knew she couldn't bear it if Clive looked admiringly at Meg. So perhaps. . . .

There was a tap at the door, then it opened and Lena came in, carrying a breakfast tray.

"Good morning, madam. I hope you slept well."

"Slept!" Luisa shrugged impatiently at the concern in Lena's long dolorous face. "Put the tray down, Lena. Put this mirror away. Look, I've got the bandages off."

"So you have, madam."

"Would you know I was the same person? Have I changed much?"

Lena looked doggedly. "You've hardly changed at all, madam. I'd have known you anywhere."

"You're not telling the truth, Lena. I don't look the same at all. No one would know me. Not even my husband if I met him at a party."

"Oh, madam!" Lena spoke chidingly, as she would to a child. "That is wickedly exaggerating."

"It's the truth, it's the truth! Where's that big photograph of me? I'll show you."

"It's gone, madam."

"Gone?"

"It was taken away. I don't know where it is."

"You mean my husband has taken it away—torn it up."

"I don't expect he's torn it up, madam. Just put it away."

"So no one will recognize me," Luisa whispered. "So the girl he met in the Borghese Gardens is gone —forever. . . ."

In the morning everything seemed much clearer to Meg, although not more understandable. Clive hadn't meant her to see Luisa. He had made the best of it when it had happened, but if Luisa had stayed in her room as she had been told to, she would have been whisked back to the hospital in the morning early, and no one else would have known about her visit home.

That could be the only reason for Clive telling no one that she was coming home last night. It was so strange that he should have got the message, and kept silent about it, only warning her to keep her door shut so that she would not be disturbed.

Now, when it was too late and Meg had seen Luisa, he was going to allow her to stay home for a little while, before going back to the hospital for the next operation. But why had he been so secretive at first? Because he couldn't bear strangers to see her injuries—injuries due to his carelessness, which had marred the beautiful face he had loved? Or because she might have told Meg that she was really Angelica?

"You are a clot!" Meg told herself impatiently. "Always harping on that theme. Even Luisa denied it, so it can't be true."

But she couldn't forget the faint catch in Luisa's voice when she had heard about the old château, weakened by shellfire, and bombing, and age, finally collapsing into a heap of rubble.

But at least all this, mysterious as it was, was intensely interesting and she realized she had woken without Derek being automatically first in her thoughts. It even felt good to be alive, to be in the country, and to be preparing for her first day's work in her new occupation.

Meg was further reassured to find that Clive really did expect her to work very hard indeed. There was no doubt he needed a secretary, for he had an accumulation of letters that would occupy them both for some time. Also, he was planning new projects, and seemed glad to have someone with whom to discuss them.

They worked all morning in the little study at the back of the house. Lena brought coffee at eleven o'clock. Her long dour face was just as disapproving as ever, and she put the tray beside Meg's typewriter without a word.

"Thank you, Lena," said Clive pleasantly. "Is Mrs. Wilton up yet?"

"She's still in her room, sir."

"That's good. I rely on you to see that she doesn't try to do too much. I've told her she's home temporarily. And if she has a relapse the doctor won't allow it again. Tell her I'll be up shortly to see her."

Clive's voice was that of an affectionate but sensible husband. It hardly deserved the flash of contempt, or was it anger, in Lena's eyes.

An hour later Clive flung down his pen. "I think that will do for this morning, Meg. Have a rest before lunch. Go up and see Luisa. It will cheer her up."

"Yes, of course."

Meg was surprised by Clive's request, and even more surprised when he went on: "Tell her about the girl you confused her with, what was her name?"

"Angelica."

"Yes. It will interest Luisa. And you say she married an Englishman, too? What a pity we don't know where she is. Hers seems like a similar background to Luisa's. They might have been real friends."

His gaze was so open and direct, it was impossible to read anything behind it. Yet something drove Meg to persevere.

"Did Luisa lose her family and home in the war, too?"

"Yes. She has no one at all. I found her living with the enormous family bed and a few pieces of sculpture and odds and ends in a very poor part of Rome. But this other girl at least had a grandmother and a villa, you said."

"Both gone, now."

"But presumably exchanged for a good husband, eh?" Clive gave his crooked attractive smile. "See if Luisa would like you to do anything for her. She might like something in the village. I want you to call on Hans after lunch with a check for the painting I sold for him. He's always hard up, poor devil. He'll appreciate getting it quickly. Ask him to let you see his studio. You'll find it quite interesting. Hans has all the mannerisms, at least, of a successful artist.

"Oh, and by the way," he added, as Meg got up,

"I've persuaded Luisa to leave the coverings off her face. She's terribly sensitive about it, poor darling, but it really isn't too bad now. I know I can depend on you"—his eyes rested a fraction longer than seemed necessary on Meg's clear unmarked skin—"to be tactful."

"I'll try, Mr. Wilton."

"Good girl. It's going to be a blessing having you here."

The telephone rang just as Meg was leaving the room.

"Answer that, will you?" Clive said.

She came back to pick up the receiver. The voice in her ear was already familiar.

"Is that Miss Burney? It's Simon Somers."

"Hullo, Mr. Somers. How are you?"

Her voice was a little guarded. Clive was listening and she didn't know yet whether she regarded Simon as a friend or not.

"I'm well. I hope you are."

"Of course."

"Splendid!" His enthusiasm seemed a little out of proportion. Hadn't he expected her to be well?

Yet involuntarily Meg smiled, then caught Clive's look of impatience and said quickly, "If you want to speak to Mr. Wilton, he's here, Mr. Somers."

Clive sprang up. "What does he want?"

The slow voice went on in Meg's ear, "Yes, I'll speak to him. I've got an old picture he might be interested in. But don't run away, Miss Burney. Or why can't I call you Meg, as other people do?"

"I can't stop you calling me anything," Meg said primly, uneasily aware of Clive's eyes on her.

"Then Meg it is. When are you going to come

and have a look at my shop? Come this afternoon and have tea."

"I'm afraid I'm working, Mr. Somers."

"Simon."

"Simon, then. Just a moment, here's Mr. Wilton."

Meg handed over the receiver. Her cheeks were pink. She hadn't come to Frenchley to fight off advances, from Simon Somers or Clive Wilton or anyone else. She merely wanted to work, and get used to a new life. Yet there was no doubt that the hint of advances were stimulating. Just good for her morale, she thought, and she gathered up her things again.

As she was going out she heard Clive saying, "It's not an original, you say? No, one would hardly expect that. What's the period? Early seventeenth century. . . . And what's the frame like? . . . Ah, now that I might be interested in. The rest, I should think, is valueless. Hope you didn't pay a lot for it. Well, I'll drop in some time. . . ."

VIII

Upstairs, Meg found Luisa sitting at her window looking out over the garden. She wore a most becoming rose-pink negligee. With her head turned away she looked young and boyish with quaintly cut tufted hair, and a long slender neck. There was no look of the young Angelica with her long black hair about that gamine head. Neither was there any look of Angelica about the face, which Meg saw as Luisa turned.

She had one hand half up to hide it. Her eyes were apprehensive and furtive. She was as wary as a badly-hurt young animal. But apart from the bad scarring Meg did not find the agonizing injuries she had been led to expect. It was an unfortunately blemished face with a look of artificiality. That was all.

"Has my husband been working you too hard?" she asked in a high artificial voice. "He can be a bully when he wants his own way."

"No, not really. He suggested I come to see if I could do anything for you."

"Lena does everything for me." The answer was quite polite, but with an undertone of hostility. She wouldn't mind plain dour middle-aged Lena doing things for her, but Meg, young and pretty and un-scarred, no.

"Couldn't I just talk to you for a little while," Meg said with quick sympathy.

"Why? Does Clive think I'm lonely?"

Again there was the stiff pride, giving away the hurt her offhandedness tried to hide.

Meg persevered. "I have to go in to the village later. I could get you anything you want."

"Oh, well. You could get me a library book if you like. Something simple. I don't understand compli-cated English books yet."

"You speak English perfectly," Meg said.

A queer sly look came into the girl's dark eyes. "As well as your friend Angelica?"

"Oh, much better."

"But if Angelica had been living in England for

two years she might very well speak perfect English by now. My husband has taught me. He has been very patient."

The unconscious softening of her voice gave her away. She was very much in love with Clive, Meg realized. And now she had to sit there looking at her changed face and wondering if it repelled him. Had she insisted on coming home from the hospital because she knew he was getting a pretty secretary? Was that why she had to come to Meg's room last night, hoping against hope that Meg might not be so pretty after all?

Luisa was not friendly, but she seemed driven by loneliness to go on talking.

"I was to learn to speak perfectly, and to dress perfectly, and then Clive was going to have big dinner parties and receptions, and be very proud of me. But then this happened. And so he has to find someone else to do those social things for him."

"Then you hadn't"—Meg didn't know how to put it tactfully—"been out in public very much?"

"No. I was to be a big surprise. To make all Clive's friends jealous and envious."

It was hard to know whether Luisa was being scathing or just naïve. There was no doubting the bitterness in her voice.

"But you'll soon be doing these things," Meg said warmly. "Really, your face looks wonderful now, and after the next operation—"

"Don't tell me lies, Miss Burney. You are to do all those things now."

Luisa didn't come down to lunch. Lena looked at Meg resentfully, and said that her mistress didn't feel strong enough to leave her room. Obviously Meg's visit had been too much for her. When she had left the room, Meg turned to Clive impulsively.

"Will you tell me, Mr. Wilton, exactly what my position is to be here."

"Why, just what I've told you. To catch up with all my correspondence. Later we'll work together in London. I explained to you that I wanted you to help at my exhibitions."

"But not at dinner parties?"

"Dinner parties?" His brows had risen slightly. "What has my wife been saying to you?"

"Oh, nothing, except that—does she think I'm to take her place? I mean, socially."

"Surely not. I expect her to sit at her own dinner table as soon as she's well."

"Then—I'm sorry, Mr. Wilton—but I think you ought to tell her. She's worrying about things."

Clive's frown, which momentarily turned his face thin and ruthless, vanished. With the greatest deliberation, Meg thought, he had removed it, and become charming and sympathetic.

"I should have realized this. The trouble, Meg, my dear, is that you're too pretty. Naturally Luisa feels it. What woman wouldn't?"

Meg was beginning to wish that she had a face as plain and uncompromising as Lena's.

"But to me she's still the lovely girl I married," Clive went on. "I suppose I've taken it for granted that she should know I feel like that. I should have told her more often. I—" he put his head in his hands for a moment. "I've been recovering, too. I've been thinking of myself too much." He looked up and his face was appealing. "Help me with this, Meg. Of course I don't expect you to take my wife's place. Together we'll have to convince her of that."

As soon as lunch was over he went up to Luisa's room. But whatever reassuring he tried to do was apparently not very successful, for just as Meg was preparing to leave the house on her errands Luisa called to her.

"Are you going, Miss Burney? Don't forget my library book."

"Of course I won't, Mrs. Wilton."

"And do take a look at the librarian, won't you? She's one of my husband's friends. He got her the position, you know."

"Really?" Meg's first feeling of uneasiness came over her. This sounded as if Simon Somer's warning might not have been such a melodrama after all. But Clive was a man of taste. He couldn't be so lacking in it as to sprinkle a small village with girls who took his fancy.

"I've never seen her," Luisa went on. "Lena tells me she's rather ugly. But I find that hard to believe. Her name's Janie Howard."

"Mrs. Wilton, don't you think you imagine these things?"

"But she's here," said Luisa simply. "That's a fact, isn't it? Oh, I'm not suggesting there's anything wrong with it. My husband simply likes decorative people about him. Now you'd better go, hadn't you?"

"Yes, I think I had. I have to call on Mr. Cromer, too."

"Hans? You're going to his studio?"

Did she imagine Luisa's slight breathlessness, the flash of apprehension in her eyes? She must have, for Luisa smiled for the first time.

"I'm sorry if I'm being unkind, Meg. I may call you Meg, may I not? Clive says I've lain in bed all these months imagining things, and I suppose I have. But don't let Hans—"

"Don't let Hans what?"

The girl's eyelids fell.

"Make you tea, if you're fastidious. He has a half-blind housekeeper, and I once saw his kitchen."

Luisa threw up her hands. Her mock horror was assumed very well, but she was covering some other emotion. It almost seemed to Meg like fear.

The narrow three-storied house that Hans lived in was in a shabby back street. All the houses were in need of painting and repair. Their doors opened on to the pavement, with low treacherous beams that caught the head of the unwary. When Meg rang the bell she had to wait some time for the door to open.

Then Hans appeared, opening the door only a few inches at first as if he expected an annoying salesman or some person who must not be allowed in. Meg had a swift impression of uneasiness. He was like a nervous cat, showing only one eye and one ear.

But when he realized his caller was Meg he opened the door wider, and became effusive.

"Why, Miss Burney. I wasn't expecting you. What a wonderful surprise. And how charming you look. Do come and see my humble place."

He was wearing a paint-stained smock. There was a smear of red paint on his forearm, and he kept his hands clasped together as if to conceal their condition. His hair was disarrayed, and there was a faint shine of perspiration on his brow.

His state of disarray, if he had come straight from his work, was to be expected. But the perspiration? Of heat or agitation? It was not a hot day. But he had hurried down the narrow stairs, of course.

Meg couldn't have said why she was so deliberately observant, or why she caught the faint atmosphere of unease.

"Mr. Wilton asked me to give you this," she said, handing him the envelope.

"What is it?"

"A check, I think."

"Oh, of course. How thoughtful of Clive. But do come in, Miss Burney. Won't you come up and see my studio?"

He had recovered himself. Whoever he had expected, the mere fact that his caller was someone quite impersonal had filled him with relief. At least, that was how Meg interpreted the now smiling welcome in his face. He looked eager and humble.

"You know already how much I want to paint you, Miss Burney. Perhaps soon you would have the great goodness to give me a little time." He flung out his hands deprecatingly. "You know, for someone with as much creative urge as I have, it is a tragedy that I don't have more ability. But I believe one day it will come. I feel it inside me. I see a face like yours and it burns me up. Oh, I talk such nonsense. But do come upstairs, Miss Burney."

It would have been unkind to refuse. Meg followed the shabby little figure—what a strong neck and head he had, and short strong arms—up the narrow dark stairs. Somewhere in the house a cat was mewing. It had a desolate sound, as if it were shut in. Or hungry.

At the top of the stairs Hans opened a door and

led Meg into the sloping-roofed studio that took up the entire top floor. There were several of his pretty Christmas card water colors on the walls. There was also a model's dais, which seemed rather ambitious, considering Han's constant protestations that he could not paint good portraits.

"Can I see one of your portraits?" Meg asked.

"Yes. Yes, by all means."

Hans rummaged among some canvases and produced an oil painting which Meg recognized as Clive Wilton, very stern and strained and lifeless, and another one of a rather buxom woman, who also looked frozen to the canvas.

"That's the barmaid at the Crown," he explained. "But you see what I mean. I can catch a likeness, but the life, the spirit, eludes me. I constantly try. You, Miss Burney, have such beautiful spirit in your eyes. Perhaps with you I would be successful."

The work was competent enough, Meg realized. But what Hans said was true. It lacked life. It was depressing and frustrating. One wondered why he persevered, or why he thought that one day the magic touch would come.

"Did you ever paint Mrs. Wilton?" Meg asked, with careful casualness.

Hans turned rather sharply.

"Why do you ask that?"

"Well, you don't seem to miss any opportunity, if I may say so. And she must have been very beautiful."

Hans seemed to be considering what to answer. Then he said slowly, "Yes, I did paint her. She was a good sitter, but the result"—he shrugged—"didn't do her justice."

"Can I see the portrait?" Meg asked. "I'd love to

know what she looked like before her accident. I looked for photographs in the house, but there don't seem to be any."

"I believe Clive had them destroyed. He thought it was better not to remind Luisa of how she had looked. The same with my painting which he insisted on owning, bad as it was. Gradually, he said, Luisa would get used to her new face. And he had her old one safely in his mind."

"But surely he must have kept one picture for himself. It's a nice thought, I suppose, but one's memory isn't as reliable as all that."

Meg spoke with some sureness, and Hans gave her a knowing look.

"You perhaps try to conjure up a lover's face, Miss Burney? I know exactly what you mean. The features elude one."

His voice was gentle and understanding, and not in the least impertinent. "But Clive is a strong minded person. This is what he wanted done. Perhaps he, too, thought he'd accept the new Luisa more easily this way. It has been such a great tragedy for them."

"She loves him very much," Meg said involuntarily.

Hans looked at her without replying. He didn't say that Clive also loved his wife. He began turning the portraits back to the wall, and at the same time the cat began mewing again in a shrill penetrating wail.

"Is that cat shut in?" Meg asked.

"Oh, it's my housekeeper's. She's gone out, and the cat always has to be shut up securely until she comes back. I don't know why Miss Burt thinks a cat so well-fed would want to escape. But she's a little eccentric, poor dear. She has fads and fancies. She's always afraid of something. Her eyesight is failing—naturally, at her age—so now she won't go out unless it's quite a gray day, like this. She thinks strong sunlight is harmful. Indeed, she's beginning to spend altogether too much time in her room, and quite neglecting the house and me."

"But you let her stay?"

"In the meantime, yes. I always hope she'll get over this phase. If she doesn't, then I'll have to send her away. She has a sister in Norfolk who might be persuaded to take her. But I won't do it unless it's quite necessary. I'm fond of the funny old creature, and I don't mind her oddities. After all, everyone has some of those. Some hide them better, perhaps."

"I think it's unkind to let the cat cry like that," Meg said uneasily. It was only a cat mewing. She didn't know why the sound seemed so forlorn and almost macabre.

"Bless your kind heart." Hans' eyes were embarrassingly admiring. "Now I see why there is soul in your eyes. I would so like to try once more to paint a really good portrait. I may arrange with Clive to give you a little time off for sittings? Please say yes, Miss Burney. You would be doing me a much greater kindness than you realize."

He looked so innocent and eager, like a little boy, that Meg said good-naturedly, "Why yes, if you really want to."

It would be very nice if Hans did produce a good portrait. His eagerness had nothing about it to give Luisa that look of apprehension. Everything here seemed normal enough, except for the cat crying so forlornly, of course—and Hans' distrait air when he had come to the door. But he was so natural and relaxed now that she might have imagined his agitation.

She wondered, as she left the house, whether she might meet the eccentric Miss Burt making her half-blind way home. But the street was empty. She walked to the end of it, then found she was going in the wrong direction. The village square, the church and the library were the other way. She could see that by the church spire towering in the distance. She had to pass Hans' house again, and involuntarily she glanced at the dark windows.

Behind the lace curtain in the little front parlor she saw a ginger cat leap on to the sill and look out. That must be Miss Burt's cat, and Hans must have let it out after all, in spite of its mistress' precautions. He must have done it because he couldn't stand the mewing. But why hadn't he done it while Meg was there?

The girl in the library lifted dark slanted eyes and looked at Meg coolly.

Before Meg could speak she said, "Don't tell me. You're the new secretary."

"How did you know?"

"Haven't you noticed the size of this place? Who else could you be?" The girl's voice was not unfriendly, but it seemed to hold some cynical amusement. "Besides, London's written all over you. I like that dress."

"You're Janie Howard, of course."

"Why of course? Don't say Clive told you about me. I don't think he was one to boast about his disappointments." Janie suddenly dropped her blasé voice, and leaned forward interestedly. "Say, can you sum him up? To me, he was just one big mystery."

"I didn't come down here to sum him up. I'm only his secretary."

"You're just as pretty as Simon said."

"Simon! Has he been talking about me?"

Janie eyed her shrewdly.

"He has, and I might add, it's not one of his habits to talk about women. So you've really made an impact."

"It seems to me that everybody talks about everybody in this place. It obviously doesn't mean a thing."

"Depending," said Janie cryptically, still eying Meg. "But you're fair. Not dark like me. I just can't make Clive out. You'd think if he liked dark women, he'd stick to them."

"I told you I'm only his secretary," Meg said with some aspersity. She looked at the girl with the tilted secretive smile and added, "What were you?"

"Oh, don't get ideas. I was nothing. I was as innocent as you. Well, not really, because you look as if you still believe in Clive's good intentions. I never did, actually."

"But you came."

Janie shrugged. "So what? He found me carrying cups of coffee in a coffee bar. He said the Frenchley library needed a young and attractive librarian. Those were his words, I promise you. He said he could get me the job if I liked to live in the country. It was going begging. I thought anything would be better than the coffee bar. And he is fascinating, you have to admit. Besides, I do like books. I started studying for a degree in literature once, but I haven't the staying power, you know. Anyway, I assure you I'm not in the least jealous."

"Jealous! You mean, of me?"

"Sure. I certainly would have been if I cared about Clive."

"But look here, you are wrong. I really am only Clive's secretary. I've been working like a slave all morning. And anyway his wife's home."

Janie sprang up. "No! She's not!"

"She certainly is. I've come for a book for her. Why shouldn't she be home, anyway?"

"No reason. Except, that no one really believed she'd come home again."

"You mean she was expected to die?"

"No. She wasn't that badly hurt. It was just that people didn't think she'd come back to Clive. Or that he'd have her back, for that matter."

"Because—she was afraid to come?" Meg said the words without meaning to. She hardly knew why they came to her mind.

"Well, there were rumors which I didn't hear until I came here. I expect you didn't either."

"About the accident being caused by Clive's carelessness?"

"Well—more than carelessness, some people said."

"But why? Luisa was so beautiful. At least, everyone says so."

Janie looked cynical. "It isn't only a pretty face a man wants. Perhaps that's all Luisa had. Tell me, what does she look like now?"

"Just different, I suppose. Really not too bad. But I'd certainly hate something like that to happen to me. She's terribly nervous and sensitive, poor thing."

"She must loathe you being there," Janie said.

Meg looked distressed. "But surely she can't think —I mean, is Clive really like that? Has hasn't even attempted to touch me, let alone make any sort of suggestion. He's really behaved just like an employer."

"You've scarcely tested him yet, have you? I bet he didn't know his wife was coming home."

Meg was silent, realizing the truth of the statement. But there was no need to admit it to Janie Howard. How much that Janie slyly insinuated about Clive was true? After all, Simon Somers had suggested the same things. But Janie herself admitted Clive had not behaved in that way with her. And remembering his face with its strained and lonely look she could not believe badly of him.

"Well, what does the beautiful Luisa want to read?" asked Janie. She stood up, her narrow voluptuous body shown to advantage in a black sweater and skirt. "Does she like romances? No, I imagine she's grown out of them, poor thing. Perhaps she'd like a who-dun-it? But no again. That might be a frightful *faux pas*."

"I think you're talking fantastic nonsense!" Meg burst out.

Janie laughed. "I suppose I am. You have to think up some melodrama in this dead place. There's only Simon and Clive and Hans to liven things up."

"Oh, Hans," said Meg. "I've just called on him. He wants to paint my portrait."

Janie spun round. Her face was brilliantly alive, her strange slanted eyes gleaming.

"You stay away from Hans!"

"Why do you say that?" Meg asked, that queer uneasiness stirring in her again. Luisa had said that, too. Or hinted at it. Yet what had there been to be afraid of in him or his shabby dark house except the mewing cat?

"Because he's mine," Janie said shortly, and unexpectedly.

"Oh, is that all?"

"What do you mean 'Is that all?' It's a hell of a lot. I've fallen for him, heaven knows why. That's why I've stayed here. That's why I wasn't disappointed when Clive fizzled out."

"He only wants to paint me," Meg said placatingly.

"That's all he wanted with me, too. But you can spend hours alone together in that studio. His housekeeper might just as well not be there. You never see her. She's crazy, anyway."

Meg laughed. "Don't be silly, Janie. He's not my type."

"Well, I didn't think he was mine, either. But then he speaks to you in that beguiling way, and he has beautiful hands. Have you noticed? Really beautiful." Janie shivered. "Oh, I guess I'm a bit daft. Clive, who's far more handsome, leaves me cold, and I fall for a failure like Hans."

In her blasé way, Janie was oddly likable, and Meg came away feeling comforted that she now had one friend here. Comforted? She turned the word over in her mind, knowing it was the right one. She had been feeling uneasy and even a little afraid ever since Luisa had come home so strangely the night before. Certainly she was Clive's secretary and the job really did exist. But there were all these undercurrents. And now Hans visualizing her on canvas as an angel . . . While Janie made no secret of her jealousy. . . .

With the book Janie had chosen for Luisa, a safe travel one about Spain, Meg went in a preoccupied way into the street. She immediately bumped into Simon Somers who was carrying a very large picture and looking a little abstracted himself.

But pleasure immediately came into his face. He stood in front of her, barring her way.

"The pretty secretary!"

Meg tried to remain cool and guarded.

"Am I just a type to you?"

He seized the opening and asked with interest, "Tell me what else you are."

"Hans thinks I'm an angel," she said lightly.

Rather to her surprise, Simon didn't look amused, or even mocking. He narrowed his eyes thoughtfully.

But all he said was: "Hans is a dreamer. He should take lessons from the old romantics and paint you with a dove in your hand, and a heavenly choir melting into the sky."

"Goodness! You should be an artist yourself. Or are you?"

Meg looked at the picture in his hand. He turned it to show her a dark cracked painting, the figures on it almost indecipherable.

"No more than this fellow was two centuries ago."

"Oh, is this the picture Clive wants for its frame? It is rather a nice frame, isn't it? When it's cleaned up it should look well."

Simon touched the grimy gilt molding.

"There are some broken bits that I imagine can be mended. Clive says he has a clever chap who does it. Then he puts a good print into the frame and sells it for a nice price. You know what suckers people are for the genuine antique, chips and all. Clive has me scouring the country for old paintings."

"Do you often find them?"

"Not often as old as this. I got it at an auction sale at a country house yesterday. The painting itself is quite valueless."

"But sometime you might pick up a genuine old master," Meg said.

"I hardly think so. Not in this commercial age. Most people know to the last penny what their stuff is worth. And Clive's much too hard-headed to indulge in airy dreams like that. Are you going back to the house now? Can I walk with you?"

"The road's public," said Meg.

"Now that I call a really gracious assent. And you looking like an angel, too. Are you going to let Hans paint you?"

Meg faced him in perplexity and impatience.

"Why all this harping on Hans painting me? First Clive, then Luisa, then Janie and now you. It seems to me he must be the most pampered artist in England. Especially seeing that he isn't even a good one."

Again she noticed the narrowed look of thoughtfulness in his eyes.

"Sit for him. It might be an interesting experience." He stopped, and seemed about to say something else, but thought better of it. After a moment he said, "But don't let him mess about with you."

"Mess about with me!"

"I'm sorry. Don't look so indignant. You're not Janie."

"Janie's in love with him," Meg said stiffly.

"Yes," said Simon, again with that odd deliberation. "So she is. That certainly makes it easy for Hans. And another thing. If you do sit for Hans, let me know."

"Why?"

"Because, believe it or not, I happen to be interested in what you do. Do you mind?"

"Is that all? Not because you, too, think Hans is perpetrating some crime?"

She had spoken lightly, and was startled by the vehemence of his answer.

"Do you think I'd let you go into real danger?"

Some forgotten warmth stirred within her. Why should this strange young man care?

"Everyone around here talks in riddles," she said. "Anyway, the place is so small, you'll soon hear what I do."

They were walking down the narrow street where Hans lived. Meg had an impulse to tell Simon about the cat shut in Miss Burt's room, but let out the moment she had left. But the incident seemed too trifling. Anyway, there was a light in Miss Burt's window upstairs now, so she must have returned to feed and comfort the cat.

It was growing dark as they turned down the track across the village green to where Clive's house stood on the outskirts of the village. Simon began asking Meg about Luisa's return, which seemed to surprise him just as much as it had done Janie. It seemed that all the gossip in the village had been directed against Clive, which was very unfair.

"And tell me," said Simon, "in spite of her changed appearance, did you still think Luisa was the girl you met in Italy?"

"I don't see how she can be. She says she isn't. Why should she tell a lie about that?"

"And you're quite satisfied she really isn't Angeline, or whatever you said her name was."

"Angelica." Meg hesitated. "Yes, I think I'm satisfied. There'd be no point in her making a mystery of that. Would there?"

"Well, none that we know," Simon qualified.

"Luisa speaks perfect English, and Angelica's was very bad, almost nonexistent. Besides, one came from Florence and one from Rome."

"So we're told," said Simon, again with his rather exasperating reasonableness. "Did Angelica have any mannerisms you noticed particularly?"

"I don't think so. I didn't know her well. I only stayed one night, and actually I remember the old grandmother better. She did all the talking. But I must admit it's strange—"

"What?"

"That they both married Englishmen. Luisa and Angelica."

"The susceptible English! Well, you'll have plenty of opportunity to get to know Luisa now that she's home. If Clive lets you, of course."

"Of course he'll let me. He wants me to talk to her, to try to keep her cheerful."

"I just thought he might keep you so busy at the typewriter," Simon said mildly.

"Must you be so sarcastic about Clive?" Meg demanded exasperatedly.

"Must we even think of him?" said Simon comfortably. "Tell me about yourself, Meg. Where's your family? How much do they love you?"

"I have a brother in India, and my father lives in a hotel in Torquay," Meg said.

"And you have a lover?"

"Is that any of your business?"

"I think it's going to be my business, you know. Whether I want it to be or not." He linked his arm in hers. His voice had lost its flippancy. For a moment the hard pressure of his arm seemed something to cling to. She saw his face above her, angular and tender.

"You may need me, Meg. Remember that. But at least"—suddenly he laughed in a carefree way, and all the mocking quality was back in his voice—"now I know why you came with Clive in this somewhat naive way. You weren't being naive at all, were you? You were just escaping from your past. Wise girl. You came in the right direction."

"Clive's," Meg pointed out.

"Oh, we'll manage to deal with him."

Meg was about to ring the bell of Clive's front door when she noticed that the door wasn't quite shut. She pushed it open, beckoning to Simon to bring in the picture. The light wasn't on. As she fumbled for the switch, unfamiliar still with the house, Clive's voice was suddenly audible from his study. She hesitated, thinking he had a visitor, then realized that he was speaking on the telephone.

"You damned fool!" he was saying sharply. "You damned fool! What possessed you—all right, I suppose I must come, blast you!"

As quick as a flash Simon had grabbed Meg's arm and pulled her back onto the doorstep. In his next movement he had noiselessly closed the door.

"Now ring the bell," he ordered.

"What do you think you're doing?"

"Keeping you out of trouble. Ring the bell."

Dazedly Meg obeyed. It was a few moments before footsteps came. Then a light flashed on, and Clive opened the door.

"Ah, Meg," he said. "And Simon with the new find. I can't wait to see this. Do come in."

His voice was bland, his manner unhurried and composed. It was only as he stood a moment beneath the full glare of the light that Meg realized he wasn't seeing the picture Simon was displaying. He wasn't seeing anything. His eyes were opaque, looking inward at something. Something that had just happened, or was about to happen. . . .

IX

Earlier that afternoon, when Meg had gone, Hans hastened to Miss Burt's room to keep that wretched cat quiet. Its crying was getting on his nerves. He opened the door, and the fat spoilt creature slid between his legs and ran down the stairs. It wasn't hungry, because there was a saucer of milk, and the remains of a sardine on a piece of newspaper on the floor. It was simply making all that noise because it was lonely. Miss Burt, in her suspicious way, had liked to keep it shut in her room while she was out. She was afraid of losing it, as she was afraid of losing other possessions, her eyesight, for instance. She was a queer old soul with a screw loose, as they said.

But the cat was trouble. Downstairs, it continued to mew in its penetrating voice, and Hans had to follow it, talking to it beguilingly:

"Poor pussy. Pretty pussy. Come then, and I'll stroke you. Come then and sit on my lap."

It seemed very important to make his peace with the cat. Even then it took half an hour to lure it into being friendly. Then it allowed itself to be picked up, and butted its large square head against

Hans' waistcoat, purring. Hans sat quietly in a chair, absently patting the cat. He was very tired. He felt as if he hadn't rested for weeks.

He sat there with the heavy cat in his lap until the room grew cold and it began to grow dark. He didn't like the dark. He hadn't since his youth when he had been forced, trembling with fear and excitement, to go out after curfew in the hostile streets looking for food. His mother and his young sisters were always hungry. They thought he was brave, and the lonely terrifying forays were curiously corrupting. And in the end he decided, with a cold cynical passion, that for the rest of his life he would take whatever he wanted whenever he could. By any means. . . .

He would bend people to his will. If he saw a face and needed that face to paint, he would somehow have it. Now he had got the new one, young Miss Burney's. It had all the qualities of which he had dreamed. Those heavenly wide blue eyes. One visualized radiance streaming from her hair. . . .

The house was very silent. Hans went up the stairs to Miss Burt's room with the cat. He didn't put the light on, and when something moved in the corner he started violently.

Had Miss Burt come in, unnoticed? Hans was sweating. He reached for the light switch and snapped it on, then gave a shamefaced laugh. A sharp wind was coming through the window, and the thing moving had only been her black coat on its hanger.

"You silly old creature! Your nose is too long, eh?"

Hans crossed to the window to draw the curtains. At the same moment the doorbell rang.

In a flash he had switched off the light and stood

tense, knowing he was a fool, and that whoever was at the door must have seen the light, and been aware that he was there.

But whoever the caller was would think it was Miss Burt's light, and everyone knew that she only answered the door when she felt like it.

He remained still.

A hammering began, and then Janie's voice, clear and confident, came up the stairs.

"Hurry up, Hans. I know you're home. I saw you at the window."

He went out of the room very slowly, taking care to shut the cat in. When he reached the front door he was as composed, he hoped, as he had been when Meg had called.

But twice in one day to be caught like this. . . . He could never stand this strain.

"Janie! *Liebchen!* What an unexpected pleasure!"

"You took long enough to come to the door. Whatever were you talking to Miss Burt about?"

"It was the other way around, Miss Burt was talking, and I was listening. She just came in from a long walk. Now she's tired, so I get my own supper tonight, I can see."

"Why doesn't she feed her cat?" asked Janie. "The poor thing's calling his head off."

"He's spoilt, that one. Janie, are you coming in?"

"Of course I am. If Miss Burt isn't going to get your supper, I am. You see, you're spoilt, too."

Hans bowed his head.

"I know I am. It's very sweet of you, Janie, but you can't stay. I have to go out."

"Out? Where?"

"Only to Clive's."

"But you were there last night."

"I know. But his wife came home unexpectedly. I have to see her. It's only right, Janie darling. Poor Luisa. She must be made welcome. Come, I'll walk home with you first. Oh, I must just tell Miss Burt I'm going."

He went to the stairs and called in a loud voice, "I'm going out for an hour, Miss Burt. I'll get my own supper when I come back. Don't you worry."

He waited a moment, as if listening, then shrugged.

"As if she would worry, anyway."

"Why don't you get rid of her?" Janie asked. "You're just too long-suffering."

In the dark narrow hall Hans saw her pale provocative little face and suddenly pulled her to him.

After a minute Janie wriggled.

"O-oh! You're hurting. You hold me as if you're scared I'll escape."

"Oh, no. I won't let you. I keep what I like now. That's something I've learned."

"Wise man." Janie ruffled his hair. She pulled her head back to look at him, and sighed. "Heaven knows why I feel like this about you. You're not very young, and you're not even good-looking. Most of the time you look like a badly treated dog. But then you touch me and"—she shivered—"it's the excitement in your hands. No one else has it. For me, anyway."

"It's hunger," said Hans starkly.

He walked with Janie to the Crown, and she persuaded him to have a drink at the bar before he left. Then he kissed her swiftly, said, "I must fly, little love," and hurried off.

By a roundabout route he went back to his own house. When he opened the door softly he winced a little at the sound of the cat still crying in loud impatience.

So Miss Burt hadn't come back—yet. . . . He had better begin to make plans.

Clive insisted on Simon staying for a drink. Whatever had bothered him, he had recovered quickly, and expressed delight with the picture Simon had brought. At least, not the picture itself, which he dismissed as a poor example of the work of a follower of Rembrandt, but the frame. It was a perfect example of early seventeenth century work, and in splendid condition. A little judicious touching up and he would use it for one of his more important old prints.

"If it's as good as that, it's a bargain," Simon said. "I only paid five pounds for it."

"My dear fellow, you'll never make money if you're as honest as that. I'd have believed you if you'd told me twenty-five. Well, charge me a decent commission. And have another drink. Did you and Meg meet somewhere? How did you get on, Meg? Find your way all right?"

"Yes, thank you, Mr. Wilton."

"And how was old Hans? Itching to get at paints and canvas?"

"Actually, he does want to paint me. If you don't mind, Mr. Wilton."

"I don't mind. I expected that. If you can be bothered to give him the time, Meg. He may even produce a masterpiece. At least, his subject will be worthy of it."

Clive smiled at her over his glass. "Don't you agree, Simon?"

"Worthy of someone better than Hans," said Simon.

"Perhaps. But I still have this intuition about Hans. I believe he's suffering from some mental block. One day it will suddenly clear away and then we'll really see something. It's a hunch I'm backing, anyway."

"And you think Meg might be the person to perform this miracle?" asked Simon dryly.

"I believe any sufficiently inspiring subject could. Meg particularly, because Hans gets very excited about her. She must have told you that herself. You know," he went on enthusiastically, "if only Hans can do this, Meg's could be the portrait to go in this frame."

"But I won't look as old as that," Meg protested. "I haven't been dead two hundred years."

She was only joking, but neither of the men smiled. Simon was watching Clive, his eyes lazily narrowed. Clive looked distressed.

"My dear Meg, what a macabre thing to say."

It had only been a joke. It was strange he didn't see it like that. Perhaps, for all his sophistication and cleverness, he had no sense of humor. Or not where jokes about death were concerned.

"I'm sorry I didn't see Hans' eccentric housekeeper," she said, changing the subject. "Hans seemed to be babysitting for her cat."

"Oh, yes, Miss Burt. The woman's quite mad. She ought to be sent away. I don't know why Hans puts up with her."

"He did say he might have to send her to her sister eventually."

"Yes, I'm afraid he will, and pretty soon, too, before she goes completely gaga."

Clive dismissed the subject and turned to Simon. "Did Meg tell you the good news? My wife is home. She discharged herself, and took us by surprise."

"How is she?" asked Simon.

"Really very well. Isn't she, Meg? I've checked with the doctor and he says a few days at home are just what she needs. She's got to start rehabilitating. She's abnormally sensitive, of course, but that's to be expected."

"Of course."

"I'm afraid I won't be able to persuade her to meet people for a little while. But she's improved enormously, and the next operation, thank heaven, will be the last. Then I'll take her away for a long holiday. She'd like to go back to Italy for a few weeks. We'll probably do that. After that," he gave a deep tired sigh, "life will be back to normal, I hope."

"So your stay here is limited," Simon commented casually.

"Well, it depends how long Luisa's next operation takes. And after we've been to Italy she may prefer to make a fresh start somewhere else. If that's the case I'll sell the house. In some ways I'd be glad to. It hasn't been particularly happy for me." He drained his glass and said briskly, "But that's all in the future. There'll be plenty of time for Meg's portrait to be painted, for instance. I'm sure she won't be sorry that she's giving Hans this one more opportunity."

There was a slight sound at the door, and a movement. Then Luisa's voice said very clearly, "Do you think we should let Meg sit for Hans, Clive? I've had nothing but bad luck since I did."

There was a faint tinkle of broken glass. Clive

swore softly as he grabbed at a handkerchief to wrap around a cut finger. Then he said quite gently, "Luisa, you startled me. Why don't you come in, darling, if you're listening to our conversation." He added reassuringly, "There's only Simon here. I've told you about him. Come in and meet him."

Slowly, but with great dignity, Luisa came in. She looked very slim and frail in a black dress. A light veil hung gracefully over her face.

"Are you one of my husband's friends?" she asked Simon. "I only ask," she added, "because I've met so few of them. Just Hans, and—"

"Luisa, darling! We'd only just moved here when you had your accident. How could you meet people?"

"Yes, I know." Luisa nodded meekly. "And before that I was learning to speak English properly. It's quite understandable. But now I can speak very well. At least the nurses in the hospital told me so. And Meg did, too."

She looked at Meg and said brightly, "Isn't it odd, Meg thought she had met me in Italy. But she hadn't. It was someone else."

"Luisa, darling! The doctor said you weren't to get excited—"

Luisa's eyes flew open innocently.

"Am I talking too much? I suppose I am. It's so wonderful to be normal—at least, to feel normal—"

Clive took her hand. "If you stay downstairs, you must rest. Sit quietly." His voice was controlled and gentle.

Simon put his glass down.

"I must go, anyway. I'm so glad to have met you, Mrs. Wilton. You look wonderful. Really wonderful."

"Do I?" The confident façade Luisa had worn slipped. Her voice faltered.

Simon looked down at her. "Don't let anyone tell you anything else."

"But you didn't see me before my accident." A look of uncontrollable bitterness crossed her face. "No one knows how lucky they are, until it's too late. Perhaps you had better look hard at Miss Burney's face, so you'll remember it, in case she has bad luck, too."

"Luisa!" exclaimed Clive.

Simon said in his slow unperturbed voice, "I've already done that. And I intend to go on doing so. Hans or Clive will probably find me on their doorsteps every day."

The slow voice surely didn't hold a warning!

Clive said with some asperity, "You'll only be welcome out of working hours. Are you off now? Meg, tell Lena to put dinner half an hour ahead, if she can. I've work to do this evening. And Luisa, you must do as the doctor said, and rest. You don't want to have to go back to the hospital before it's necessary."

Was Clive dispensing warnings too? His face looked thin and tight, as if he were holding himself under control. He didn't look directly at Luisa. Meg had a strange feeling that if he did the hidden anger would blaze in his eyes. He hadn't wanted Luisa home yet, and her visit was not being a success. But why?

The only comforting thing about being home, Luisa thought, was the way Lena fussed over her. Now, her long gloomy face curiously maternal and tender, she got Luisa undressed and into the filmy black nightdress, and the fine pale pink bedjacket.

Then she tucked her into bed, and said, as Clive had done ten minutes earlier: "You must rest, madam. Already you're overexcited. Going downstairs like that. Meeting strangers. You've got to be more patient."

Luisa twisted her fingers around her thin bare wrists. Her eyes had a dark secret look.

"I wanted to. And I'm glad I did. Is that young man in love with Miss Burney?"

"I'm sure I don't know. I wouldn't be surprised. All men can see sometimes is a pretty face."

"It's nice to be loved," said Luisa wistfully.

"You've plenty to love you, madam," Lena said gruffly.

"Have I? Even with my face the way it is? I wonder how Miss Burney would like it if. . . ."

"If what?"

"Oh, nothing. She's lucky, I expect. It wouldn't happen to her. Tell my husband I'd like to see him, Lena, please."

When Clive came in a little later she knew he was very angry indeed. But she didn't care. She felt defiant and reckless and satisfied. She had got back at him for the trick he had played on her this morning with Meg's bracelet. She was sure it had been a trick.

Or had it. . . .

Her eyes clouded uneasily. Then moved away from Clive's furious gaze.

If only he would, somehow, convince her that he still loved her. That he didn't, like Simon Somers, want to look unceasingly at pretty unmarred faces like Meg Burney's and Janie Howard's. . . .

"I'm sorry, darling," she murmured.

"What *made* you do it? Did you take leave of your senses? Saying those things about Hans, for instance. He could sue you for defamation of character."

Luisa put her fingers to her face, resentfully. "Well, it's true. This dreadful luck did happen to me after he painted me. And I had that queer feeling about him. You know I did. He frightened me."

"Luisa, you're simply overimaginative and hysterical."

"Oh, Clive!" Her defiance and her satisfaction were melting away beneath his angry regard. "Don't look at me like that. It was all perfectly harmless. And if you knew the courage it took to go downstairs, to meet a stranger. . . ." Her voice died away. "But you don't understand that at all, do you? You're never nervous. Never afraid."

Clive gave himself a slight shake, as if deliberately ridding himself of his anger, and some other tension, and smiled at her quite gently.

"Poor little one! I do understand. Really. But don't do it again. It isn't amusing, having people think you're eavesdropping."

"I was," Luisa admitted. "But I'm sorry. I do promise not to do it again."

"Good girl. Now let Lena bring your dinner, and then go to sleep. Dream of our trip to Italy in a few weeks."

Luisa sat up eagerly. "Are we really going? Do you mean that?"

"Of course I mean it. We'll go and take a look at your old home."

"Oh! Do you think it's still there?"

"Of course it's still there. Even if only lizards live in it. We'll be lizards ourselves for six weeks."

"Oh, Clive! If I could believe that."

"You can believe it, if you're good. As good as you promised to be. Not like tonight."

"I promise, Clive. Really I do." She told herself that she believed him and that he was being genuinely sympathetic and affectionate. She couldn't go on living if she didn't believe that.

When Clive came down to dinner Meg noticed that he looked quite exhausted. He scarcely spoke, and made a bare pretense of eating. As soon as the meal was over he sprang up, asking her to excuse him.

"I've some important work to do."

"Can I help, Mr. Wilton?"

"No. Get an early night. Your turn will come tomorrow."

If she had searched for months for a way to get over an unsatisfactory love affair she could not have found a more effective one, Meg reflected. In the two days she had been here she had been alternately so interested, so mystified, and, more than once, so startled, that there had been no time for regrets or sadness. She didn't even have any inclination to write to Derek. Let him wait, she thought.

There was probably something immensely significant about her attitude. Simon, no doubt, would analyze it accurately. But she was really too tired to do so. It had been quite a day. Since she was not likely to be disturbed by anyone prowling in her room tonight, she expected to sleep soundly. She wouldn't even ponder on the strange urgent conversation she and Simon had overheard Clive having on the telephone. He had promised to go somewhere, and had sounded angry and alarmed. But afterwards he had done nothing about it, and had behaved as if nothing had happened.

Something had happened however, for Meg thought she had been asleep all night when she was awakened by the sound of a car driving very slowly and quietly up to the garage.

The garage was immediately below her window. Her curiosity took her out of bed to look out. The time, she noticed by the luminous hands of her clock, was three-thirty.

The garage doors closed with the softest of clicks, and Clive appeared in the dim light. He stood a moment as if he were not sure of what he was doing, then walked fumblingly, as if he were drunk, round to the back door.

Interested, but a little disturbed, Meg went back to bed. This was none of her business, but she couldn't help lying listening for footsteps on the stairs. None came, although half an hour passed.

She began to worry. Was Clive ill? Had he fallen asleep downstairs? It probably didn't matter if he had, except that she was sure he would prefer not to be found by Lena, with her face of doom, in the morning.

Then suddenly she heard a dull heavy bump.

He must have fallen down! That was enough to send Meg, dragging on her cotton housecoat, flying down the stairs.

"Mr. Wilton!" There was a light on in the study, and she went there, whispering urgently, "Mr. Wilton, are you all right?"

Clive was sitting at his desk. He had a whisky bottle and a glass in front of him. His face was white, his small usually alert and attractively bright eyes, quite dull. There was a chair lying on its side in the middle of the room. He had obviously stumbled against it, and that had made the bump Meg had heard.

When he saw Meg his face stiffened. Whether he were drunk or not, his voice was perfectly steady, and full of low furious anger.

"What the devil are you doing here? Spying?"

"I heard a noise. I thought you might be ill." Meg had winced at the word "spying." That had been the last thing she had thought of.

But Clive was obviously more than a little drunk. He didn't know what he was saying. It was foolish to take offense.

"I'm not ill, and I don't want attention. You'd better go back to bed."

"If you're sure—can't I make you some coffee?"

Clive put down his glass with a small thud. Suddenly Meg was remembering how, earlier in the evening, a fragile crystal one had splintered in his hands when Luisa had come in. He was full of some inner tension. Even drinking hadn't relieved it.

"No, you can't, thank you. You're my secretary, not my nurse."

"I'm sorry," said Meg stiffly, backing away. Nevertheless, something in that taut figure held her. He was obviously suffering so much, whatever it was about.

Her instinct was right, for all at once his hostility seemed to lessen.

"I'm all right, Meg. Get back to bed. And you might not mention this to anyone. I've been driving, as you probably know, and without a license that's a criminal offense."

"Did you have to?" Meg couldn't help asking.

"No, I didn't have to. At least, the compulsion was merely moral." He hesitated, then said tightly, "I've been out to the place where I had the accident—where Luisa was hurt."

"Oh!" Meg's quick sympathy took her towards him. He smiled faintly.

"Luisa's coming home brought it all back, rather. But it's better now. You're a nice child, Meg."

He had come to stand beside her. He was close enough to take her in his arms if he wanted to, to kiss her. They were alone and not likely to be disturbed. It was the slightly eerie and lonely hour of night when comfort at least, if not love, might be sought.

If he were the kind of womanizing person Simon had tried to tell her he was, he would have done so without hesitation.

But he made no move towards her, and didn't even seem to be seeing her, although the anger had left his face. He was still looking inward, at something else. . . .

X

Simon rang the next morning. Meg was in the study, and took the call. This time he was reasonably discreet, and asked her if she were alone.

"I am at the moment."

"How's Clive?"

"I haven't seen him this morning."

"I just wondered if he had a late night."

"How did you know—" she stopped abruptly. Instinctive loyalty to her employer made her say, "I haven't any idea."

"Oh, come, Meg, you can't tell me you didn't find out about that. I don't underestimate your intelligence, or your curiosity."

Meg lowered her voice. "It really isn't any of our business what Mr. Wilton does. Anyway, I can't talk to you now."

"No, of course you can't. But I'd like to see you. Can you get out later?"

"I might. But not to gossip about my employer," she added.

"Then just to see me. There are a million things we have to talk about besides Clive Wilton."

"What are all these things we have in common? You flatter yourself."

"Do I?" His voice sounded wistful. "Then perhaps I can interest you in a fifteenth century rocking chair? Or a Georgian soup ladle?"

Meg laughed and relented. "I'd love to see them. But you'd better forget it today. I'm busy."

"Are you going to Hans'?"

"It depends on Mr. Wilton."

"Go, if you can. Have a talk with his housekeeper. Ask to see her if she isn't visible. And make sure Hans shows you what he's painting."

"Simon, you really are the most inquisitive person."

"Sorry, Meg dear. It's an idiosyncrasy I have. Let's say I enjoy it."

There were footsteps on the stairs. Meg said hastily, "I have to go."

"I understand. Clive approaches. I'll see you later. And Meg!"

About to put the receiver down, a different note in Simon's voice held her attention.

"Take care."

Then he had hung up first, and she had to smooth the baffled look from her face as Clive came in.

"Who was that?"

"It was for me, Mr. Wilton." Seeing his frown, she added, "It was only Simon Somers. He's becoming rather a nuisance."

She didn't know why she had added that somewhat coy explanation. Was she trying to protect Simon, or to deceive Clive?

Whatever it was, her ruse had succeeded, for Clive's face cleared.

"Can't blame him, Meg. But I can't have him monopolizing you."

"You don't need to be afraid of that, Mr. Wilton."

Clive sat down at his desk. He looked quite normal this morning, and showed no sign of his exhaustion and distress of some hours earlier. He was well-groomed and bright-eyed and full of brisk assurance.

"Well, let's do some work, shall we? Then you might have time to give poor old Hans an hour or so this afternoon. But he's not to monopolize you, either. By the way, Meg, I don't need to ask you to say nothing about last night. Apart from driving without a license, I couldn't let Luisa know about it."

"Of course not," said Meg warmly. "You can trust me, Mr. Wilton."

That promise meant that Simon's curiosity would go unsatisfied. And serve him right.

But it didn't explain who Clive had been talking

to on the telephone last night, and why he had said with that angry desperation, "You damned fool!"

Hans said to Janie, "Don't bother to put the dress on today. I've just one or two finishing touches to do to your face."

"You mean you don't want any more sittings?"

"That's right, my darling."

"But I can still come here, Hans?"

Hans, in his paint-stained smock, stopped work to look at her in astonishment.

"But of course. Who said you only came here for me to paint you? I love you, *liebchen*."

Janie gave her slow, tilted smile.

"That's all right, then. I thought when you started on Meg you mightn't want me."

"What nonsense is this you're talking? I wasn't going to make love to Meg, was I?"

"How do I know? I don't know how much I trust you."

"As to that, I am perfectly trustworthy. But as to painting portraits—" Hans stared broodingly at the work on his easel. Suddenly he made a passionate movement, and began to splash paint over the canvas.

"Hey, what are you doing?" Janie cried in alarm. "You're not ruining my portrait?"

"It was ruined already," he said sadly. "It doesn't do you justice. Not one little bit. It is terrible."

"You haven't even let me see it!" Janie protested.

"You can see it now, if you like."

"Oh, Hans!" Janie looked at the paint-smeared mess. "And after all that time. And the special dress and all."

"Yes. As you say, after all that time."

Hans' shoulders slumped despondently. "I don't know why I go on trying."

"Oh, cheer up, darling. Perhaps you'll do better with Meg."

"Perhaps I will. Perhaps I won't mind so much about her. With you, it had to be no less than perfect."

Janie hugged him, pulling his face down to hers.

"You old silly, I don't mind if you're not that good. But don't let it eat you like this. If you're not a famous portrait painter, you're not, and what the hell? I still love you." She kissed him, and went on, "Don't you think we ought to get married?"

"Married?"

"It's what people do occasionally. Mind you, I haven't wanted to before. I've liked having a good time. But I don't know—I keep getting this feeling that I might lose you."

Hans was still deeply despondent.

"Maybe you should, little Janie."

"Why? Because you're not going to hit the headlines? I never said I wanted to marry a notorious character, did I? Anyway, it's time you were properly looked after. I'll bet Miss Burt never got your breakfast this morning."

Hans gave a half smile. "No, she didn't. She's staying in her room today."

"Oh, really! Why don't you get rid of her? All right, perhaps you can't afford a decent housekeeper, but I could be one for nothing. I'm quite good at cooking."

"Janie, this is something—I'll have to think about it. You mean you would really like to marry me?"

"You do understand English, don't you? It's what I've been hinting at for the last six weeks. You old goof!" She kissed him on the forehead, feeling the faint dampness of emotion there. Dear Hans, he got so tied up about things. Perfectly simple things, like having the same woman for the rest of his life, rather than different ones haphazardly.

"You think about it all you want," she said reassuringly. "But think the right way."

Janie ran into Meg as she was leaving Hans' house.

"Hi!" she called in a friendly voice. "You're wasting your time going up there. Hans has just destroyed my portrait. He said it wasn't good enough."

"Did you see it?"

"I caught one or two glimpses. Hans doesn't like you to look too much. I must say what I saw looked rather odd. But perhaps he'll do better with you. Anyway, it will give him so much pleasure."

If she was wasting her time, Meg thought, why did everyone tell her to do this. Clive, Simon, even Janie. It seemed to be a social obligation to sit for Hans and keep him happy.

And Hans himself, after being a little distrait, when he was obviously thinking of Janie's visit, became full of an excitement that made his eyes glow darkly. He spent a lot of time arranging Meg's pose.

"Tomorrow," he said, "I'd like you to wear a very simple white dress. Have you got one?"

"Yes. A sleeveless white linen. Will that do?"

"The very thing. How long can Clive spare you today?"

"There's no hurry. We're going to work again this evening."

"Good. We'll have tea later. You shall help me make it. My housekeeper is staying in her room today. It's too bright a day for her eyes, she says, although the sun is scarcely shining. All I can do is leave her meals at the door, and see that she doesn't starve, poor thing."

"You mean she won't come out at all?"

"No. Though she may later, because I notice she's been feeding the birds from her window. That's a hopeful sign. She doesn't do it in her worst moods."

"She's let her cat out," Meg observed, looking at the great dark orange creature perched on a pile of old canvases, and watching her with great golden eyes.

"Oh, yes. It makes too much noise shut up. I had to insist on that. Now, Miss Burney." Hans stood at his easel staring at her concentratedly. "We'll go on talking quite naturally. I want your face mobile and expressive. So perhaps you'd like to talk about yourself? Every young woman likes to talk about herself, I think."

"I have a quite uncomplicated past."

"Nobody's past is uncomplicated to themselves." Hans' eyes were shrewd. "Yesterday you were recalling a familiar face. Of a lover, yes?"

"Oh—just someone I was fond of."

"And something happened? He left you, you left him? Or are you still good friends?"

"We haven't quarreled," Meg said stiffly.

"But you're not happy about it, of course. It's never easy when one is young. Were your family sad about your unhappiness?"

"They knew nothing about it. I don't live with them. I've only a father and a brother. My brother's

113

been in India for years, and my father's married again. Neither of them needs me. We go our own ways."

"And very wise, too. One has to grow up. And grow up out of first love as well as other things. I think this young man wasn't worthy of you."

Meg was surprised at the slightness of her pain. Hans was right. She must have been growing out of Derek for a long time without realizing it. She was going to recover. Life was going to be interesting and full of possibilities again.

"That's better, that bright light in your eye," said Hans, working swiftly.

"Janie says you destroyed her portrait."

"Yes. It wasn't good enough. Janie has a very special face. I tried hard. But it was another of my failures."

"Like Luisa's?"

"Oh, that was a little better. Even I can admit that. But not good enough. Although Clive was very polite about it. But it would have been an embarrassment to him to keep the picture, of course. Luisa's accident gave him an excuse to destroy it without hurting my feelings."

Meg found his intense humility irritating.

"Don't be so pessimistic at the beginning, please."

Hans sighed and shrugged. "You are quite right, Miss Burney. I must not be so pessimistic. This painting might be my triumph. Now, if you would lift your chin a little. Please say when you get too tired. Then we'll have tea."

Later, after she had sat for an hour, they made tea in the cold dark kitchen. Meg insisted on washing the considerable accumulation of dirty dishes, privately thinking that Hans was very foolish to let such a state of affairs exist in his house. Then she carried the tray up to the studio while Hans left a smaller one at the closed door of Miss Burt's room.

He knocked loudly. "Miss Burt! Your tea! And how do you feel now? Are you able to come out?"

Hans' voice was sympathetic and patient. Meg was a little amused and a little saddened by the small parody. For Miss Burt didn't bother to answer Hans' thoughtful inquiry, although Meg could hear her moving about in the room. Something clattered, as if she were really blind, and groping her way. But the door didn't open while Hans was there.

He came on up to the studio.

"She'll come for it presently. She doesn't like to be seen in this state. I told her you were coming, and that has made her even more elusive. If that is the right word." He gave a small humorous smile. "Miss Burt feeds the birds, and I feed her, like a great bird herself. Life is very strange."

Strange in this house anyway, Meg thought, and found herself just as inquisitive as Simon had been about the elusive Miss Burt.

"Can I talk to her through the door? Or she might let me in, since I'm a woman. How do you know she isn't really ill?"

"You can hear her walking about, can't you? No, she isn't ill, except in her mind. If she gets worse this time I've decided I'll have to send her to her sister. I can't take the responsibility for her any more."

Meg was not surprised to see Simon waiting at the end of the street when she finally left Hans' house. She had guessed he would be watching for her. Though why she should be pleased about it, she didn't know, since it was obvious at this moment that his attention was not for her alone. He had other things on his mind, his interest in Clive's nocturnal activities, for instance, and now the progress of Hans' work.

Nobody in this village seemed quite what he was. . . . Except Miss Burt, blundering about her room, like a great bird. And she Meg hadn't seen. . . .

Simon was having a conversation with an elderly woman, but when he saw Meg coming he broke away, and strolled towards her.

"Well, angel?"

"Don't you call me that, too!" Meg begged.

"Is the theme growing a little monotonous? How is the maestro?"

"All right."

"And the preliminary sketches?"

"He preferred me not to see them."

Simon nodded, unsurprised. "You should have insisted. I told you to."

"Why? What would that have proved?"

"I expect you're right. Nothing, as yet. How good a judge of drawing are you?"

"I'm not a judge at all."

"Pity," said Simon briefly.

"Simon, what is this? You constantly waylay me and throw questions at me. It's becoming embarrassing."

Simon grinned, his eyes glinting amusedly.

"Did you see Miss Burt?"

"No, I didn't."

"Did you try to?"

"Her door was locked. I did try it when Hans wasn't watching. I had only a minute. But it was locked." Meg looked up at his face, now sober and thoughtful. "Did you think she wasn't in her room?

Because she was. I heard her walking about. And her tea tray was taken in. But the cat was in the studio," she added thoughtfully.

"I've just been talking to the neighbor across the road," Simon said. "She can see partly into Miss Burt's room. She says she can see the old lady standing there. But she never seems to move. On the other hand," and now Simon seemed to be weighing up evidence, "the birds had been fed on the windowsill as usual. The old lady has a streak of sadism. She feeds the birds so that her cat can spring at them."

"But the cat wasn't in the room," Meg pointed out.

"So you tell me."

"All the same, Simon, this is none of your business. If Hans wants to put up with an eccentric, that's his affair. What happens in his house is his affair."

"Yes, you're quite right. And if Clive wants to call late at night to pick up some of Hans' masterpieces, that's his affair, too."

"Is that what he was doing?" Meg exclaimed.

Simon laughed heartily. "Caught you that time. So Clive was out, and you were interested. But fair enough, if you don't want to talk about it."

"It's his business!" Meg insisted. Nevertheless, that faint intuitive apprehension had touched her again. She was suddenly seeing Clive sitting, exhausted and haunted, in the study early that morning. If he had only been shifting pictures, why had he been so upset? But perhaps one of them had been the portrait of Luisa, the one Hans had said was quite good. . . . Perhaps he had taken it away somewhere secret.

Simon touched her arm. "I don't know what

you're thinking, but it can't be any more fantastic than what I am."

"No!" she whispered. "What is it?"

"Old Hans is a Bluebeard. He begins to hate the women he can't paint to his satisfaction, so he carries them away in sacks."

In spite of realizing it was one of Simon's peculiar jokes, a shiver went over Meg.

"You clot! That isn't particularly funny. And where does Clive come in?"

"Yes, where? That's the puzzle." And the utter seriousness of Simon's voice was the most disturbing thing of all.

But in a moment he was saying lightly, "Come and have a drink with Janie. She'll cheer us up."

Janie was at the bar of the Crown, and very ready to cheer them up. She had had several drinks, and there was a becoming flush on her high cheekbones.

"I've done it," she said. "I've proposed. Can you imagine? I, who said all fun and no ties, and that I'd have to be dragged to the altar."

"Janie, not to Hans!"

Janie looked at Simon, pouting a little at his voice.

"Who else? You say that as if you disapproved."

But Simon's reaction had been momentary. He shrugged and said lightly, "You go on your own sweet way. It's none of my business, as Meg is constantly pointing out. But do tell us what answer Hans gave you."

Janie giggled.

"Oh, he was a bit startled, the sweet. But what answer can a man give, anyway? He could hardly have the bad manners to refuse." Janie swallowed her drink and giggled again. "I'm going back presently to clinch the deal. I don't know what we'll live on, of course, until Hans paints his masterpiece. I'll have to stay on at the library for the present."

"You've got it all worked out," said Meg.

Janie nodded, her eyes bright with happiness.

"I'm still practical in some ways, even if you wouldn't think it. But gee, I never thought I'd fall for someone like Hans. Human nature has some queer tricks up its sleeve, hasn't it?"

After another drink with Meg and Simon, Janie was very loath to spend a dull evening at the library changing books for a lot of dull people who wanted to gossip about the church fête, or their latest illnesses. Besides, she couldn't wait to see what Hans was going to do about her proposal. She supposed she could hardly expect him to come rushing ardently up to the library to accept her. He wasn't that kind of person. Whatever dreadful things had happened to him in his youth had taken his confidence away. He would make love to her, of course. He couldn't help himself about that. But as for taking the initiative in making any permanent arrangement, he was just too slow and shy. She would have to do it again. And it might be as well to waste no time about it. After twenty-four hours of cool thinking, there was every chance Hans' caution would win. Most likely he would say he was no person to take on the responsibility of a wife. How could he even support her?

She had her answer to that. They were two people alone in the world—she had only some distant cousins living in Scotland—and the main thing was to have each other, not success and money. She loved nice things, of course, pretty clothes and smart cars, and good restaurants. She had always planned to eventually marry a man who could give her those things. But now she discovered she didn't really want them—not as much as Hans and his deep slow voice and his caressing hands.

It shouldn't really be so hard to convince him of that. Not now it was evening and they would have the house to themselves, except for the loony Miss Burt who never interfered. Janie began to shiver with anticipation and excitement. Or was it just that one drink too many?

She gave her tilted self-mocking smile. Silly Janie, she'd always known how to look after herself, but here she was going in the deep end over a penniless foreigner, ready to do anything. . . .

There were no lights showing in Hans' house, but Janie knew he was home because the front door wasn't locked. After waiting in vain for him to answer the bell, she tried the knob and found it turned.

But it was strange that Hans hadn't answered the bell. She was just faintly alarmed. Of course, he may be out and only Miss Burt there. She hadn't thought of that.

"Hans!" she called softly. "It's me, Janie. Are you home?"

There was a muffled sound from somewhere. It sounded like someone sweeping with a hard broom. Miss Burt taking a fancy for a little housework, Janie thought. And about time, too.

But there were no lights on. Was Miss Burt blundering about with a broom in the dark because she wouldn't trust her eyes to the light? Really, that mad old woman would have to be sent away. Janie went up the stairs, determined to take this matter into her own hands. She was certainly not going to share a house with such an eccentric. Hans was too easy-going altogether.

"Miss Burt!" she called. "Can I come in?"

She switched on lights recklessly, and then saw that the door to Miss Burt's room was standing wide open. The room was quite quiet, and looked empty. The sounds she had heard must have come from the kitchen or the basement.

But now she was here she would make sure Miss Burt wasn't hiding behind a door, like the silly old creature she was.

She went in reaching for the light switch.

"This won't hurt your eyes, Miss Burt. If you're here, I want to talk to . . ."

Her voice died away. She stared at the dark figure in the window which hadn't turned, the shabby black coat, and the shabbier black hat, perched on her head, indoors. . . . How funny, keeping her hat and coat on, especially when it wasn't likely that she had been out.

"Are you all right, love?" Janie faltered.

She groped unsteadily for the light switch.

There was a clatter on stone stairs below.

"Who's that?" came Hans' voice, hoarsely.

Janie began to giggle with a touch of hysteria. So it was Hans in the basement with the broom. Poor Hans, doing his own housework, while upstairs his housekeeper stood like a scarecrow in the dark.

"It's only me," she called in a fair imitation of Miss Burt's quavering falsetto voice. "I wondered what you'd fancy for your supper, Mr. Cromer. I'm just coming down."

(And if silly old Miss Burt was listening there in the dark, serve her right. It was time someone told her a thing or two.)

Hans came blundering up the stairs. Janie caught a glimpse of his curiously distraught face, and, giggling wildly, found the light switch in Miss Burt's room.

The light flooded on, and she flew inside, shutting the door against Hans.

"Sorry, Miss Burt," she said breathlessly. "I didn't mean to. . . ."

Her voice died away.

For the dark figure of Miss Burt in the window hadn't turned. There was just the back of her shabby black coat, her tall shabby black hat perched on her head, at a slight angle, as if she were drunk. . . .

"Is anything wrong?" Janie began uncertainly.

The door opened behind her. It opened with a slow strange deliberation.

"That will be enough, *liebchen*," said Hans, very quietly.

Miss Burt's coat swung slightly in the draught from the open door. Her hat tipped sideways, revealingly. . . .

Janie was only dimly aware of being caught as she fainted. . . .

XI

Although it was mid-morning, Meg found the library closed. Sent by Clive, who said he had a lot of telephoning to London to do and wouldn't require her for some time, she had come to change Luisa's book.

The woman in the shop next door heard her knocking and put her head out.

"You won't find anyone there, miss. Miss Howard left."

"Left!"

"That's what I hear."

"But she can't have. I was talking to her last night and she had no intention of leaving then."

"Well, she's gone. Sudden-like, isn't it? Caught the first train this morning, as far as I hear. They say she's been jilted by that foreign artist. So she just packed her bags and up and left." The woman's sharp eyes went over Meg. "Can't be surprised, really. You city girls find it hard to take to a small place like this. Makes me wonder why you come."

"We come to work," said Meg shortly.

"Aye. Well, there'll be no books for anyone today. Mr. Clegg can't get another girl as quick as that. He's pretty mad, I can tell you."

"But last night Janie was so happy. I just don't believe this."

"You go and ask at the Crown where she stayed. They'll tell you."

The landlady at the Crown, the same pink-cheeked buxom person whom Hans had painted, was very ready to talk.

"You're not the first asking, Miss Burney. Mr. Somers has been in, too. He's just as puzzled as all of us."

"But did she say why she was leaving in such a hurry?"

"Oh, yes. She was in tears about it, poor thing. Seems she was in love with Hans Cromer, and thought he'd marry her, but he wouldn't. You can never trust these foreigners."

"I wouldn't have thought Janie would have set all that store by marriage," Meg murmured. "Not enough to run away in a huff."

"It was more than a huff, Miss Burney. I think they'd quarreled. I told her to sleep on it, and she'd feel better in the morning. But she said she was determined to go. What was there to stay for? The sooner she got out of this place the better. My husband said she went early this morning, by the first train. By the way, are you happy out at the Wilton's?"

Meg looked at the woman in surprise. "Quite happy, thank you."

"It's only that there's a room going now, if you'd have liked it."

Meg's brain worked quickly. "I'd like to see it."

"Of course. I'll take you up now. Excuse the state it's in. We're short-handed. Rosie won't have got around to doing it yet."

That was exactly how Meg wanted to see the room, the way Janie had walked out of it at first daylight. She didn't know exactly why she expected to find something there that would be important for her to know. And there was nothing, anyway. A small room that looked inexpressibly dreary with the unmade bed and the signs of a hasty departure.

A book lay on the bedside table, marked at the place Janie had stopped reading. There were hairclips on the dressing table, and a handkerchief crumpled into a damp ball on the floor.

But Janie's bags and clothes, and Janie herself was gone. There was no doubt of that. She had packed in a hurry, and in a tearful state of emotion. One would not have thought her the type to run away, but she had.

Meg stood at the window and found herself looking down into Simon's antique shop. The light was on, and she could see him moving about inside. Suddenly she felt immensely grateful for his sanity. She realized that she must take her vague alarm about Janie over to him, and be reassured.

"Thank you, Mrs. Martin," she said. "I think I won't decide to move just now. But thank you for letting me see the room."

As they went downstairs into the bar, the landlord called.

"Is that Miss Burney you've got there, Leila? Did you give her Janie's letter?"

"I didn't know she left one."

"Sure she did. She gave it to Rosie to give Miss Burney. It's here."

He took the letter, where it had been propped against a soda syphon, and handed it to Meg.

Meg found herself unwilling to open it in face of that pair inquisitive eyes. She thanked the two of them again and went out. Straight across the road into Simon's shop, as if a magnet drew her there.

"Simon, Janie's gone!"

He gave his sudden warm smile that expressed, in that moment, only pleasure at her appearance.

"Hullo, Meg, darling. How nice of you to call on me. Yes, I knew Janie had gone. She caught the six-fifteen train this morning. I inquired from the railway porter."

"How did you know to go to the station? Were you following her?"

"Not me! I'm not accustomed to getting up with the birds. I merely checked up later."

"Because you didn't believe she would run off like that either."

"No. I thought she had more staying power. I didn't even think one man could upset her that much. She's an attractive little slut, you know. But

Hans must have scared her off completely. She did leave by the early train and she was alone."

"You thought Hans might have been with her?"

"At first I thought he might have persuaded her to run off with him. But he hadn't. What's that letter you've got?"

"It's one Janie left for me."

"Then open it!" Simon said impatiently. "Here we're guessing at probabilities, while you've the answer in your hands."

For no reason she could think of, Meg found her hands trembling as she opened the letter. But disappointedly she found that the scrawled writing told her nothing. It merely said:

"Dear Meg,
    Keep away from Hans. For your own good, believe me.

                                        Janie."

There was an immense blot across the writing. It could have been a dropped tear.

"Well?" said Simon, watching her with his intent brown eyes.

She knew what he was asking. Was she going to take Janie's warning seriously? The warning of a jealous girl.

"Does she really think I'm interested in Hans personally?" she said, with scorn. "Anyway, if he doesn't want her, she'll have to forget him."

"So you think that's what this means," Simon said. "Merely that she's jealous."

"What on earth else would it mean?"

"I'm not sure. Are you game to find out?"

"Simon, you're being ridiculous. I came in here expecting you at least to show some common sense."

126

"What I'd like," said Simon, with apparent irrelevance, "is a word with Miss Burt."

"You mean, to cross-examine her about Hans and Janie?"

"About several things," said Simon thoughtfully. Then he ran his fingers through his hair, pushing it back absently. "I think I must simply have a melodramatic turn of mind."

"But what is it you're thinking?" Meg was bewildered and impatient. "Anyway, Miss Burt is mostly locked in her room and I never see her."

"But is she really there, do you think?"

"Of course she's there. I told you. I heard her walking about. And you said the neighbors could see her through the window."

"Yes, I did." Simon smiled suddenly. "Well, if she's there, she can't stay there forever, can she? I wonder, by the way, if she locks herself in, or if Hans does it for her."

"If Hans locked her in," Meg said patiently, "how does she open the door to get her tray of tea?"

"Yes, of course. Unless he unlocks the door for a minute or so. Only then she might try to escape, mightn't she? It's all quite goonish, isn't it? When are you going there for another sitting?"

"I'm supposed to today."

Simon came to put his hands on her arms.

"Keep your eyes open, but if you get nervous— even a little bit nervous, don't stay."

"Simon, you're not suggesting Janie ran away because she was scared!"

His fingers pressed into her arms. "There's something more than a little odd going on. I've suspected it for some time. I feel it's rather important for more

127

than one person to find out what it is. The only way to do that is to get into the house. And here, you're the only one who has the entrée."

Meg looked at him with widened eyes, unwilling to believe what he was suggesting, yet knowing she had had more than one presentiment of danger herself.

"I wish I could do it instead of you," Simon was going on. "But I'll be around. You can always find me here. You will come to me, won't you, Meg?"

"*In extremis,* of course." She tried to speak lightly. "If I'm able to."

"Of course you'll be able to," he said harshly. "I'm not suggesting you're in any physical danger. But I'd also like," he added, "to have you come because you wanted to."

"If I mustn't trust Hans or Clive, why should I trust you?"

He dropped his arms to his sides. He had begun to laugh softly.

"You flatter me, Meg. I'd never imagined being a sinister character."

Sinister! What a word to use! Nevertheless, the vague disquiet was washing over her again, making her heart miss a beat.

"It may be the right word. I don't know. We'll find out, I expect. But you might make an issue with Hans about seeing Miss Burt. Tell him you won't believe she's there unless you see her."

"The footsteps. The cat. The tea tray gone," Meg pointed out. "Hans is a magician, I suppose."

"He may well be. But to the devil with Hans. Janie, too. I'm just putting the kettle on. Stay and have some tea. You've scarcely looked at my shop. Isn't it a fascinating heap of junk?"

Meg looked around the dark low-ceiling shop, with its array of miscellaneous articles, china, glass, silver, chandeliers, brass helmets, rusty swords, gargoyles and even a grinning and enormous ship's figurehead.

She picked up a rosy Venetian goblet. "Everything isn't junk. This is precious."

Simon smiled in appreciation. "You have an unerring eye. Are you interested in antiques?"

"I'm crazy about them."

Simon looked touchingly pleased. "And in addition you decorate the shop. That goblet looks twice as beautiful when you hold it."

The reflective tone of his voice warmed her.

"I'm not planning to stay here permanently."

"I wish you were." He came towards her. His eyes were on her lips. She knew that he was going to kiss her.

For a moment Derek's face was very vividly in her mind, with a sharp feeling of regret. Then it had gone. This young man, for all his casual air, seemed to have a peculiarly dominating quality. It was as if he were firmly thrusting Derek aside.

She moved away, as he went to take her in his arms.

"No," she said instinctively. "Don't do that. How am I to take you seriously, any more than Hans or Clive?"

His arms dropped. He looked hurt.

"I've taught you to be suspicious."

"For my own good, I'm sure."

"Very much for your own good. As far as Hans and Clive are concerned, anyway. And the kettle's boiling. So will you trust me to make you a cup of tea?"

There was no opportunity, after all, to see Miss Burt, for that day Hans had sent her to her sister in Norfolk. He borrowed Clive's car to drive her to Maidstone where he put her on a train for London. He had telephoned her sister, who would be at Victoria station to meet her. He explained to Meg, when she called at his house later, that Miss Burt had got beyond managing.

She had never stayed in her room for more than a day at a time before, but this time she had refused either to come out or to speak for nearly a week. Indeed, when Hans had made the arrangements with her sister, he had had to almost forcibly take Miss Burt down to the car and help her in. The neighbors would verify this, for one of them had called out asking if he needed help.

He had refused this, in case Miss Burt should be further agitated, and by that time he had persuaded her to get into the car without further protest. He had thought he might have to take her all the way to London, but by the time they reached Maidstone she had thrown off her peculiar mood and returned to sanity. The change and excitement had brought her back to normal, and she insisted that she was perfectly able to travel alone.

"After all, she only had to get out of the train at Victoria," Hans explained. "She couldn't make a mistake about that. A child could do it. And really I felt I'd done my duty by her in going to all this trouble. I'm only thankful I got her away while she was able to go at all. I'd let her stay here too long, poor old creature."

Meg listened to the silent house. There were no footsteps in Miss Burt's room now. She had never seen the old lady and she had a queer feeling that

130

she had never existed. The birds had been fed on the window-sills by an invisible hand and unseen feet had clumped on the floor.

"So now you've lost both Miss Burt and Janie," she said. "You knew Janie had gone, didn't you?"

Hans gave his expressive shrug. He looked hurt and sad.

"Janie also became unmanageable, I'm sorry to say."

"Didn't you care about her, Hans?"

"I liked her very very much."

"Then what did you do to make her go so suddenly?"

"We both lost our tempers," Hans said reluctantly. "Janie took it too seriously." Then he went on exasperatedly: "Women want too much! They frighten me. I suppose I was unkind to poor little Janie. I didn't want to be. But she brought about this situation herself, with her unreasonable demands. I had to be frank with her. Well—" again he shrugged. "Life goes on. Janie will be all right. She knows how to take care of herself."

"But aren't you a little sorry?" Meg persisted. Was his attitude of philosophical regret too simulated?

A look of anger, so fleeting as to seem imagined, passed over Hans' face. It had come and gone so quickly that Meg had had only a glimpse of what Hans, when really angry, might be. Then he said in his gentle hiding voice, "Now, Meg dear, let's not get personal. That way everyone gets hurt. I just want to paint your face, not to hold post-mortems."

Meg was a little ashamed of her blatant curiosity. She had listened to Simon too much.

"I'm sorry, Hans. It's none of my business."

"That's all right, my dear. Everyone will talk, naturally. Just as they talked about Clive and poor Luisa."

"But Janie isn't hurt!"

"Ah, no. Not physically, anyway. I was just indicating that this is a talkative village. Now, while the daylight lasts, I must work."

Overnight two women had disappeared out of Hans' life. There was nothing to prove that there had been anything mysterious about their going, yet Meg was overwhelmingly conscious of some sort of menace. In the quiet house? In the silent staring cat who had seen everything, but told nothing? In Hans himself who looked preoccupied, the lines carved deep in his face?

Meg said she couldn't stay long because she had had an hour off in the morning, and although Clive had told her to come, he wanted to do some more work before dinner.

"Then we'll have tea early," Hans said briskly. "Actually, I find my mood is wrong today, too. Too many things have happened. I thought work would calm me, but I'm only going to do it badly." He threw down his brush. "You stay here, Meg, while I make tea."

"Can I do it for you?"

"No, no, you talk to the cat. He's lonely, now that he's lost his mistress."

Meg stroked the cat's round golden head. But he was an aloof creature, and gave no sign of pleasure. He sat on an old wooden trunk, his paws neatly folded under his chest. The afternoon sunlight shone in his eyes, making them blaze. It shone, too, on the dusty window panes, and the unswept floor, and caught a glint of red fire on some material that had caught in the lid of the trunk.

Meg was suddenly eying it with an unevenly beating heart. She couldn't explain her intense uneasiness in Hans' studio this afternoon. It was as if some sorrow or fear remained in the air.

Janie had had a red dress, she remembered, a slim tube of material that had accentuated her voluptuousness.

But Janie had left Frenchley. Everyone knew. The people at the Crown, even the station porter had verified that fact.

Yet Meg was suddenly cold with apprehension. She tipped the cat roughly off the chest, and then was afraid to lift the lid.

When at last she did so, she gave a small exclamation of relief, and then of admiration. For the red material was merely part of the skirt of a brocade gown, a really beautiful gown made in medieval style. There were the shoes, and the small black cap, and the heavy ropes of pearls to go with it.

Hans must use these things as props for his work. Poor Hans, with his high ambitions. Filled with excitement, Meg suddenly decided to put on the gown and the pearls. Quickly, before Hans returned.

The stiff material crackled. The waist was almost too small. She held her breath and secured the hooks. The black velvet cap sat demurely on her pale hair. She moved stiffly towards the dais where she sat to pose. The cat watched her unwinkingly. Hans had wanted her to wear pure white, but she felt much richer and more vital in this heavenly old dress. Hans would agree when he saw her.

She sat with her back to the door waiting for him to come.

Presently teacups tinkled, and the door was pushed open.

"Here we are—" Hans began, and stopped abruptly.

Meg kept her back to him, not moving. Then, when there was no more sound, she looked round, laughing.

"Did I surprise you? I found this lovely—Hans, what's the matter?"

"Take it off!"

Meg stood up uncertainly. She couldn't understand his grim unamused face.

"But I thought—are you angry with me?"

"You all pry!" he burst out. "All of you! That dress was in a trunk. The lid was shut. You found it. How? Where else have you pried?"

"Nowhere," said Meg stiffly. "The material was sticking out under the lid. It looked such a heavenly color. I'm sorry if you didn't want me to see it." She looked at his set face, and added coldly, "If I'm to take it off, you'd better leave me for five minutes."

But with some immense effort of self-control, he had recovered himself. He put the tea tray down and gave his familiar philosophical shrug.

"I'm sorry, Meg. It doesn't matter whether you see the dress or not. I was just upset for a minute. I thought you were Janie."

"Oh! Did Janie use to wear it?"

"She tried it on once. She looked wonderful. She has the face of that period. You must have noticed."

"Hans, you do love Janie!" Meg exclaimed. "Then why ever did you let her go?"

"I know. It was all my fault. We quarreled. I hurt her badly."

"Perhaps she'll come back."

"No. She won't come back. And it's all for the best. We'll both get over it. It wouldn't have worked, her marrying me."

"But why, Hans?"

With another of his bewildering changes he snapped: "Would you mind not asking so many questions about things that don't concern you. And now take off that damned dress!"

He went out, and Meg slowly undid the hooks. She found that her fingers were trembling slightly. She suddenly envied the cat, watching unmoved, the angry words flying over his head, what he saw meaning nothing. For surely it wasn't sadness that made Hans' face so gray, so curiously crafty. . . .

XII

Luisa came down to dinner that night. She wore a simple black dress, and had obviously spent a long time over her hair and face. She looked almost beautiful. There was a timid sparkle in her eyes, giving a hint of the vivacity she must once have had.

Tonight the ghost of Angelica looked out of the marred face. Meg was convinced of it.

But suddenly she didn't want to probe any more. She was afraid of what she might find. She kept hearing Hans' voice, oddly final, saying, "No, she won't come back."

He talked of Janie. But had he once said it of Angelica, and instead of Angelica a strange young woman called Luisa had come back?

"You are worrying about something, Meg?" Luisa said in a perfectly friendly voice.

Meg started. "No."

"You've been so busy all day, I've scarcely seen you. Shall we have a drink without waiting for Clive? I'm feeling so much stronger today. It's wonderful to be behaving like a normal human being again. Will you have sherry, or something else?"

"Sherry, thank you, Mrs. Wilton."

Luisa poured the drink and handed it to Meg.

"There! I didn't even spill. My hands used to tremble so much, but they're better now. Oh, did you get my library book for me?"

"No, I'm sorry. The library was closed today."

"Today? But it's Wednesday. Is Janie ill?"

"No. Actually she's left."

Meg spoke casually, wondering why she watched for Luisa's reaction. She was getting wary of everybody.

"Apparently she and Hans had a quarrel. She was very upset. So was Hans, I think."

Remembering Hans' behavior, Meg didn't immediately notice the apprehension in Luisa's eyes. But her white face and her sudden stillness became very obvious.

"Where did she go?" she asked tensely.

"I don't know. London, I expect."

"You mean—she might not have gone at all?"

"Oh, yes, she went. She really did catch a train."

"You—you know that?"

Why had Luisa's careful poise suddenly left her? Why was she the uncertain frightened girl again? Meg noticed the sherry slop over a little from her glass. Her hand was trembling again.

With deliberation, she said, "Miss Burt has gone, too. Poor Hans. So now he's left with no one."

Luisa's eyes, enormous and alarmed, were on Meg. But before she could make any reply, Clive's voice had come from the doorway. "Are you girls gossiping about Hans again? But you must know he doesn't really care for anything but this obsession he has about his work."

Luisa spun round. Her voice was urgent, and strangely appealing.

"Clive, did you know Janie had gone?"

"Who doesn't? This is a small place."

"And Miss Burt?"

"Of course. I told you Hans was borrowing my car, don't you remember? He should have got rid of that crazy old woman weeks ago."

"You didn't tell me," Luisa said in a low voice.

"Darling, I did. Just before lunch. I told you not to be surprised if you heard the car, it wasn't me driving. Perhaps you were asleep."

Luisa looked at him silently. She didn't contradict him again, but her gaze was unbelieving. Presently she said in the same low voice, "And where has Miss Burt gone?"

"To her sister in Norfolk, or so Hans says. She was being met at Victoria. Hans put her on the train. And might I add, darling, it's nothing to do with us. Or are we going to gossip like the rest of this village? I've had trouble enough with old Clegg already about the unreliable person I recommended for the library. He intends to have a local girl next time. Meg, you'd better have another drink, because I intend to keep you working late tonight. After all you've had most of the day off."

"Have you been sitting for Hans again, Meg?" Luisa asked, and now there was no mistaking the tenseness in her voice.

"Just for a very short time. Hans seemed too upset about Janie to concentrate. And then I was stupid enough to put on Janie's dress—"

"Janie's dress!" Luisa's eyes were wild and dark. "What do you mean?"

"Oh, just a heavenly old brocade Hans had been painting her in. You didn't think I meant Janie's real dress, Mrs. Wilton? Where would he get that?"

"Oh, of course," Luisa exclaimed. "How silly of me. Just for a minute I thought"—her apprehension was very obvious—"something must have happened to Janie," she finished lamely.

"My darling, your nerves are still in a very bad state," Clive said with concern. "All that's happened to Janie, I imagine, is that she's escaped being seduced by Hans."

"But that was one thing she didn't want to escape," Meg said involuntarily.

She had gone too far. Clive said politely, but with ice in his voice, "I hardly think your brief acquaintance with Janie, Meg, warrants that opinion. She's a very shrewd young woman. She'll play her cards her own way."

"What cards has she to play?" Luisa's voice was full of a strange fatality.

Clive went to her and kissed the top of her head.

"I think you don't quite follow the English idiom, darling."

"Perhaps I don't. But tell us, Meg, what Hans said when you wore the old dress?"

"He said it was Janie's, not mine," Meg said flatly.

She found she didn't want to remember Hans' gray face. "He wants me to wear white."

"Don't go back into his house alone," Luisa said suddenly and passionately.

Clive's eyebrows went up. He began to laugh in genuine amusement.

"My darling, you flatter Hans. Is he so dangerous to women? Well, I suppose only women can answer that question. What do you think, Meg? Could you go overboard about him? The way Janie has, for instance?"

"You're being stupid!" Luisa hissed. "You know I didn't mean that."

Clive took her hand. "And I think you're a little overtired. Look, your hand is trembling. Lena!"

The dour housekeeper couldn't have been far away, for she appeared immediately, her face expressionless. Eavesdropping, Meg thought.

"I think, after all, my wife ought to have her dinner upstairs."

"Yes, sir. I said that all along, but she would come down."

Luisa was pouting. The look of a scolded child had come back into her face.

"Run along, darling. I've a present I'll bring up later."

"A present!"

"Something you've been wanting for a long time. I was going to give it to you just before you went back into the hospital, but tonight seems as good a time as any. If you're good, of course."

Clive spoke as he would to a loved child, and Luisa responded in a childlike way. She showed first the love of an unexpected present, and also the hope that perhaps after all she had pleased her husband, and he still loved her. But there was another completely unchildlike emotion beneath her pleasure. Meg tried to interpret it. The intense questioning look she was giving her husband suggested suspicion.

But this place was riddled with suspicion and false rumors. She was tired of them.

"Well, Meg, another drink," said Clive when they were alone. He poured himself a substantial whisky. "As you see, my wife is very far from well. She gets extraordinary fancies. I can't think why she's taken this dislike to Hans. I'm sure he hasn't lifted a finger to hurt her. Metaphorically speaking, of course. I can only explain it by the fact that he was one of the last persons to know Luisa's face as it was before the accident. I think this gives her a subconscious resentment against Hans. He wanted to paint her then, but not now. So she's hurt and jealous when he paints other women. By the way, he doesn't affect you in any peculiar way, does he?"

"N-no," Meg said slowly. Again she didn't want to remember the vaguely sinister atmosphere of Hans' house, or be like Luisa and exaggerate it. "But strangely enough," she added, "Janie left me a note telling me to stay away from him."

She saw the quick interest in Clive's face, concealed in a moment of deliberate amusement.

"More melodrama?" he asked lightly.

"Just jealousy, I should think. Poor Janie."

Clive swallowed his drink. His face was smooth and empty.

"The subject of Janie is becoming rather monotonous, don't you think? At this moment she's probably having dinner with some likely person she's picked up on the train, and all this nonsense about a broken heart is an invention. Janie's the complete extrovert."

Of course, Clive had picked Janie up in a coffee bar himself. He dismissed her as being the easy come, easy go sort. He was probably right. The reason for the passionate little note she had left—*stay away from Hans for your own good*—was just something Meg was too perplexed and too tired to work out.

Simon would do it for her. The thought of Simon brought a surprising warmth and reassurance to her. He would get to the bottom of what was going on. . . .

Luisa wasn't asleep when Clive came upstairs three hours later. She had stayed awake waiting for her present. She hadn't allowed herself to think of anything at all except what it might be. Not her apprehension about Hans and Janie, or Meg with her open innocent face. The thought that Janie might be lying ill somewhere with a badly injured face was only the edge of a nightmare. She had been imagining things for so long now that Clive was quite right, she could scarcely tell reality from dreams.

But Clive had a present for her. That was real.

Lena came in to see if she needed anything.

"You should be asleep, madam. I'll put the light out."

"No, don't. I'm not tired. I'm waiting for my husband."

"He's working with Miss Burney," Lena said in her grudging disapproving voice. "How do you know he won't go on until midnight?"

"Never mind. I'll wait. He's coming up because he has something to give me."

"Then why does he keep you waiting like this?" Lena asked bluntly.

Luisa stubbornly would not allow her anticipation to be spoilt.

"He knows how I love anticipation. Go away, Lena. You're worse than the nurses at the hospital."

Lena huffily tidied the room and put fresh water in the jug beside Luisa's bed.

"I try to look after you, madam, but all the good's undone."

"Yes, Lena, I know you look after me. Sometimes I think you're—the only one—who does." The treacherous words came out involuntarily. Luisa was immediately sorry for them, and said impatiently, "Oh, go away, Lena. I'm perfectly all right. And my husband will be up in a moment."

It was almost midnight when he came. She knew that he had deliberately kept her in suspense. But the sight of his slim neat figure and his alert smiling face did the usual things to her. She knew that if the present, whatever it was, had to be paid for, she would pay. Not because she was in such a frail state of health, but because she was forever caught in his frightening spell.

"Still awake, darling?" he said in his concerned voice.

"You promised me a present, Clive."

"Oh, but of course. What a child you are, Luisa. You couldn't even wait until morning."

"You promised it tonight."

"So I did, and you shall have it."

He took a slim square package from his pocket and tossed it to her.

She opened it eagerly, and then exclaimed in disappointment: "Oh, it's just the bracelet for Nurse Green."

"No, for you. I have another for Nurse Green. Not quite such an expensive one, because naturally you must have the best. Well, darling"—he came to sit on the edge of the bed—"do you like it?"

Luisa held up the gold chain with its jingling charms.

"Oh, Clive! Is it really for me? It's what I've always wanted."

"As you've showed me on two regrettable occasions," Clive said softly.

Luisa's eyes flew up to meet his. "But now I won't do that again—now I have one of my own. If you'd given me a bracelet like this at the start I wouldn't have been tempted. And honestly, I'm certain I didn't take Meg's. . . ."

Her voice died away beneath his calm regard.

"I wanted you to try to overcome that weakness, Luisa. But you didn't, did you? Never mind, we'll say no more about it, provided you go on being good. Minding what you say, for instance."

So there was a reason for the bracelet. He hadn't given it to her from love and affection. Her face went stony.

"You mean about Hans, don't you?"

"Hans is my friend. I don't care to hear you saying strange things about him."

"I didn't say anything."

"I apologize. You merely insinuated. But that's just as bad. Because you don't like him doesn't mean you've got to suggest he's an ogre."

"Why does he have to paint Meg?" Luisa muttered. "And where's Janie? Where is she?"

"Janie's in London. I happen to know."

"*You* know!"

Clive gave his wide charming smile, the one that had made her heart turn over in the sunny Borghese Gardens so long ago, in another life, it seemed.

"Darling, Janie's nothing to me, as I've told you often enough. But I do know she's gone back to London, and it's quite true that she went in a huff with Hans. So stop worrying about her. What's she to you, anyway? Once you hated her because you thought I was attracted to her."

"Weren't you?" Luisa whispered.

"In a purely friendly way, which seems to be something women can't understand. Really, darling, do I have to persuade you all over again that you're the only woman I love? And the sooner I can get you out of England back to your own country and sunshine, the better. Then I have such great hopes the girl I fell in love with will be in my arms again. She will, won't she, my sweet?"

Luisa jingled the bracelet on her wrist. Its smooth cool feel filled her with a sensuous pleasure. She concentrated on that, and on Clive's tender ardent face. He really did mean what he said. She was certain he did. She would forget Janie and Meg and the queer menace of Hans, and her next ordeal in the hospital, and think only of the sun shining on olive trees and faded tawny houses, and the beloved sound of her own language.

"You do mean all this, Clive?" she asked passionately. "You will keep your promise? Even if the next operation doesn't do all we hope?"

"I'll keep my promise"—his eyes held hers—"if you keep yours. No more foolish talking."

Luisa nodded willingly. He kissed her gently, and

then with warmth, his lips clinging to hers for a long time. It was the first time he had kissed her like that since the accident. After he had gone she lay for a long time savoring the exquisite pleasure.

But before she fell asleep the unhappy doubts had crept back.

Why hadn't he given her a simple thing like a gold charm bracelet which he knew she hankered for long ago? Had he withheld it from her hoping she would succumb to that overwhelming kleptomaniac impulse, so that then he could extract promises from her . . .?

The tears were still wet on her cheeks when at last she slept.

Simon seemed as determined to deal in cryptograms as everyone else. The next morning Lena gave Meg an envelope which she said Mr. Somers had left for her. He had wanted to see her, but Lena had told him she was busy with Mr. Wilton and couldn't be disturbed.

Lena's long face expressed its usual disapproval. But she was honest, as Simon must have known, and would discharge the task.

The envelope contained only a newspaper clipping from the local newspaper published that morning.

It was headed "Mysterious Find" and went on:

"Last evening two schoolboys made a strange discovery in an overgrow ditch some ten miles from Maidstone. What they thought was a body proved to be nothing more sinister than a dressmaker's dummy. Its origin and how it came to be there remains a mystery. Has some home dressmaker with too much *avoirdupois* finally despaired and tried to lose proof of her once slim figure? Or has someone simply been cleaning out an attic? We suggest a little more tidiness with this kind of debris."

Simon had written underneath only, "The mad Miss Burt? Or am I madder?"

XIII

As soon as she had the opportunity Meg went flying into Simon's shop.

"You are mad, Simon. You must be. Why ever do you say an extraordinary thing like that?"

Simon grinned welcomingly. His face was full of pleasure. "It's one way of getting you to come and see me, at least."

"But Simon, you must be joking. You can't mean that fantastic thing."

"It is fantastic, isn't it? But it could explain Miss Burt's strange lack of animation. Hans had to practically lift her into the car, so the neighbor said. She offered to help, as I told you, but Hans said he could manage. Now if that were the real Miss Burt, and she refused to help herself, how could Hans have lifted her into the car unassisted? But a dressmaker's dummy, wearing Miss Burt's very distinctive old black hat and coat, is another matter. It would require nerve, of course, but not too much physical strength."

Meg had gone rather pale.

"Then where *is* Miss Burt? She's not in her room, because the door's wide open. And the cat sits in the studio. . . ."

"How good are you at acting?" Simon asked.

"Acting? Now what is it you want me to do?"

"Can you assume another voice for any length of time?"

"Oh, yes, easily. I always played the eccentric in school plays."

"I don't want you to play the eccentric now. I merely want you to ring up Hans and say you're Miss Burt's sister in Norfolk. Tell him Miss Burt arrived safely, and is well and happy. Something like that. Keep your ears skinned for his reaction."

"But, Simon!" Meg whispered. "If you think—whatever it is you're thinking—shouldn't you go to the police?"

"About a dummy found in a ditch? They'd think I was pulling their legs. How are things up at the Wiltons, by the way?"

"All right. Except for undercurrents, of course. I get the feeling that Luisa's scared of her own shadow, but I can't think why. Clive says he's taking her to Italy after her next operation. I do hope it will be a success, because then she'll be almost good-looking again. She's so sensitive about it. I think her only chance of happiness is if she gets her looks back again."

"Italy," said Simon reflectively. "I wonder why."

"I suppose because that's where Luisa wants to go. It would make her happy."

"Have you ever thought for one moment that Clive Wilton would put a small thing like his wife's happiness before his own interests?"

"Now what are you suggesting?" Meg asked exasperatedly.

"Darling Meg, if you married me, I'd take you to the South Pole if it pleased you. But we're talking of Clive who is quite the most coldly ambitious man I've ever met. If he's taking Luisa to Italy, he's doing it for a reason that suits himself more than her."

Meg sat down on an old dusty rocking chair. "I give up. I think I'll go back to London."

"What to?"

She opened her eyes wide. "Are you talking of me now, not Hans or Clive, or Luisa or Janie, or a dressmaker's dummy called Miss Burt?"

"I'd talk of you all the time if you'd let me. What would you be going back to? Another job, less mysterious but much more dull? Someone who's waiting for you? Tell me. I want to know."

In spite of herself, Meg could not keep up her casual attitude. "No one's waiting for me."

He searched her face. "Does that make you very unhappy?"

Did it? She found she was thinking of Derek with nothing but mild remembered pleasure. Not with any bitterness at all. How long must it have been since she had used him all unwittingly only as an object for love, because that was a very necessary thing for a girl to have? But the thought of being completely alone was not so pleasant.

"I can manage," she said in a low voice.

He put his hand over hers. "You could try with me what Janie tried with Hans. You might find me more responsive."

"Oh, Simon! Be serious. This is hardly the time. We've other things to think of."

For answer he pulled her to her feet, and into his arms.

"Nothing is more important than this," he said and kissed her before she could resist. It was not the affectionate but somewhat passionless kind of kiss Derek used to give her. Indeed, it was sweeping away Derek's lingering shadow and urgently demanding response. . . .

After a little while she said breathlessly, "Simon, do behave! We're in full view of the street."

"Who cares?" His arms were closely around her, possessive and loving. "This is what I wanted to do yesterday and you wouldn't let me. So now I shall take my time." He kissed her again. "Don't go back to London, Meg."

"I wasn't really planning to," she admitted.

"I don't like you in Clive Wilton's house, and I loathe to think of you in Hans' studio. But I think you'll have to go just once more. It might be rather important. For Janie and Miss Burt. Luisa, too. After that, I promise you, we'll think of no one but ourselves. But in the meantime, let's try this telephone call to Hans. Then you can go straight up to him and watch him recovering."

Meg drew away from Simon, apprehensive again.

"What are you really thinking? Because I can tell you, Luisa's frightened of something, too. I almost decided last night that I wouldn't sit for Hans again. There's something sinister about his house. But if you really think it's important to Janie and Miss Burt. . . ." She searched his face. "Or are you just thoroughly enjoying playing the amateur detective?"

She saw the lightheartedness had gone out of his face. It had a grimness that was not just assumed. She said slowly, "All right. I know myself there's something very odd."

"Good girl, Meg. Just remember I won't be far away. Now give me fifteen minutes to get up to Clive's, then ring Hans. Say that since he was so good to your poor sister, Miss Burt, you think he might be worrying as to whether she arrived safely."

"And she did?"

"She did."

"Why are you going to Clive?"

"Don't ask questions. I'll meet you at Hans' house in about half an hour. Tell him you're sorry you can't sit for long today because I'm calling for you."

"You just want me to see how he looks? Or what he's doing?"

"That's all."

Meg's heart was beating rapidly as she put through the telephone call to Hans. She had to take a deep breath before she could answer his gutteral voice. He sounded more foreign over the telephone.

"Who is there, please?"

"Is that Mr. Cromer?" Meg spoke in a quick high voice.

"Yes, this is Mr. Cromer speaking."

"Oh, Mr. Cromer," she began garrulously. "I'm so glad to hear your voice. I just wanted to tell you Elaine arrived safely yesterday, thanks to you."

"Elaine?"

"My sister, Miss Burt. You kindly put her on the train. I wanted to thank you for your patience and understanding with her. She's really very difficult, isn't she? I had no idea."

"Is she?" Hans' voice was vague, almost inaudible.

"You must have put up with it for a long time. She says you've been very good to her."

"I don't know what you're talking about. Who are you, anyway?" Hans' voice was suddenly a shout. Meg jumped and held the receiver away from her ear.

"But I told you, Mr. Cromer. I'm Miss Burt's—

Elaine's—sister. I'm ringing to say she arrived here safely yesterday."

"Arrived. . . ." Now his voice had sunk to a thick whisper. Then abruptly the telephone clicked. He had hung up.

Meg was shivering violently. The success of the call had not filled her with triumph but with pure dread. She would rather have done anything than go round to Hans' house. But Simon had said it was important.

She straightened her shoulders, picked her way out among the multiple articles in Simon's shop, closed the door behind her and set out.

When she rang Hans' doorbell he did not immediately answer it. She thought she could hear his voice within. Then there was the distinct ping of the telephone bell, and after another moment or two the door opened.

"Ah, Meg! I thought it would be you. Don't you find it very hot today?" He was mopping his brow. He didn't look at her directly. He was very busy ushering her in and closing the door so that in the dark little hall she couldn't see his face clearly.

"And a good thing you have come because I may have to go away. I must have one more sitting to do justice to you. I should have several more. But this is impossible—impossible."

"Have you had bad news?" Meg asked solicitously.

"Yes. A friend in Amsterdam. A very close friend. You see, I have no family, which makes me value friends all the more."

But not Janie, Meg thought. You let her go. . . .

"What will you do with the cat?" she asked irrelevantly.

"The cat?" He looked at her blankly. She realized he had scarcely heard anything she had said. Now fear touched her with the coldness of ice. Why was he so deeply upset by that telephone call? So upset that he was on the verge of panic.

"Oh, someone will take the cat. It's a nice cat."

"Didn't Miss Burt want to take it with her? Or wasn't she in any condition to?"

The dressmaker's dummy clutching a cat to its round bosom! Meg had an hysterical desire to burst into peals of laughter. She realized that Hans was giving her a long side-long look, full of some secret contemplation. She tried to speak lightly.

"By the way, I can't stay long. Simon is calling for me in half an hour."

"In half an hour! What work can I possibly do in that little time!"

"I was only doing this to oblige you, Mr. Cromer," Meg said stiffly. "I don't have to sit for you. And it really isn't convenient today."

She was dreading going upstairs, past Miss Burt's door to the low-ceilinged studio. But something was impelling her. She had to see this adventure through. She couldn't weaken now. Simon would be ashamed of her. And she had the feeling of being on the verge of a deeply important discovery.

"But you must make it convenient for a little while, I beg you!" Hans was saying. "There's so little time. And I did want to do a much better job of you. It's infuriating to have to hurry it. But let me get what I can done."

Meg began slowly to walk up the stairs. She made herself talk politely and naturally.

"You look upset about your friend, Mr. Cromer. Are you sure you will be able to work?"

"I can work at any time," he answered ferociously. "My work is all I have and it comes first. Before friends, before any people at all." Then he tried to smile, shrugging off his intensity. "Now you see why Janie left me. I am a great big ogre, yes?"

His smiling face belied his words. But they were true, Meg thought. Behind his deliberate smile she was aware of another expression, that of someone dangerous, perhaps a little crazed. It was what Luisa had been trying to warn her about. The ogre hidden within him. . . .

Clive himself opened the door to Simon.

"Hullo, Simon. What can I do for you?"

"Have you got time to chat? I think I'm on the track of another painting."

"Genuine?" asked Clive.

"I hope so."

"Come in. I can't give you long, I'm afraid. I'm expecting some calls from London."

Simon followed him into the study. He sat down, stretching his long legs comfortably.

"By the way, what date did you decide the last painting was?"

"Late eighteenth century."

"Oh, no. Seventeenth, surely."

Clive raised his eyebrows, smiling. "I won't argue with you, but I'm certain it's eighteenth. Anyway, as you know, the painting itself is incredibly bad, and quite worthless. The frame, on the other hand, is remarkably fine. If you can lay your hands on an earlier one, I'll certainly be interested."

Simon mentally noted Clive's emphasis on the later date of the picture. He was lying, of course. He knew his stuff even better than Simon did. And

Simon was aware that his own knowledge was not small. Apart from the proof that could be given by experts' examinations and X-rays, he knew that canvas had been late seventeenth century.

But Clive, for some reason, chose to deny it, although the earlier date would have added to its value.

"Where's this new picture?" Clive asked.

"Hadston Hall. There's not much of value left there, but this is one thing I have my eye on. The sale is next week."

Simon stopped talking as the telephone rang.

"Interesting," commented Clive, picking up the receiver. "Excuse me a moment, Simon. This will be my call from London. Hullo! Hullo! Yes, this is Clive Wilton. Oh, it's you. I didn't recognize your voice for a minute. You sounded—what's that?"

Simon was lighting his pipe. He didn't appear to be watching Clive's abrupt movement away from him, turning his back, the receiver clamped to his ear.

"But that's impossible! You're imagining things!" His expostulation was completely spontaneous. But in a moment he had recollected himself, remembering he was being overheard. His voice became low and calm. Simon couldn't help admiring his self-control. "I can't talk to you now. This must be gone into. I think you're under a misapprehension, you know. You've been working too hard." He paused a moment, listening. Then he exclaimed sharply, his agitation unconcealable, "Oh, soon, you fool! Keep your head, if you can."

He replaced the receiver, his hand lingering on it for a moment before he turned back to Simon.

154

"Sorry. What were you saying? Oh, look here, old man, I'm really rather tied up, and now one of my men seems to have messed up a deal. Come and see me when you've more details about that picture. I may not be interested. I'm not plnning to do much buying at present. I intend taking my wife away for a short holiday."

"I thought you were going to do that after her next operation."

"Yes, I was. But these skin grafts take an infernal time. A little time abroad would do her good. If I can persuade her to travel in her present state."

Simon stood up. "I expect you can persuade her to do anything."

Clive looked at him sharply. His face seemed to have grown smaller, almost wizened, definitely monkeyish now, even to the bright-eyed suspicion.

"What makes you say that?"

"Don't tell me you don't know what a woman in love will do for a man."

"Oh, well, yes. Luisa does love me, bless her. In spite of everything."

The man was a consummate actor. But humility was out of character. Simon spoke casually, covering his dislike.

"Then you seem to have got Miss Burney down here on false pretenses."

Clive's eyes flew open so briefly that the animosity in them might have been imagined.

"I don't have to account to my secretary for my change of plans. Besides," he added suavely, "Meg will understand. She's a nice person."

By that time, Simon hoped privately, Meg would understand completely. He took a leisurely farewell.

But when he was out of sight of the house he began to run. He knew now what he had to do, and there was no time to spare.

Luisa heard the front door bang. A little later Clive came upstairs.

"Who was that calling on you, darling?"

"Just Simon. Taking up my time when I've none to spare. I've a surprise for you."

Luisa sat up eagerly. "Another? What is it?"

"We're going to Italy immediately. We're not going to wait for your next operation. I've just been having a word with Doctor Lennox on the telephone. He thinks it a splendid idea."

But Luisa shrank back nervously.

"Oh, Clive, no! I can't travel like this. Oh—but I'd love to," she finished wistfully.

"Now don't be absurd. Of course you can travel. You'll wear a veil, and no one will notice a thing. The sun will do wonders for you. Doctor Lennox agrees. Besides, I have to go anyway. I'm on the track of what might be a very important find. Very important indeed. I've just had a call from London about it."

Luisa looked up into his vivid face. He was very excited, she could see. He was irresistible when he was like this, sweeping all difficulties aside. It was how he had been when she had protested about marrying a stranger so quickly. He had said that anything could be a success if one's heart was in it.

And her heart could genuinely be in this sudden extravagant scheme. To see Italy again, Florence as old as time, the familiar faded roofs and towers, the olives and cypresses, the hills melting into the summer sky. . . .

But would he let her see Florence? And was this trip for her, or for the important find, whatever that was?

"Don't you want to help me, darling?" he was asking. "Apart from doing you a world of good, it will help put other dealers off the scent if I appear to be just on a holiday with my wife."

"Will they believe that any more than I do?" Luisa asked cynically.

His expression was deeply hurt.

"Luisa! What a thing to say! Why, we talked of this trip before I'd even heard of the picture."

"Hadn't you?"

"No, I swear I hadn't. I told you, I've just had a call from London. Darling, don't make difficulties. I want us to catch the late plane, tonight, if we can. So there isn't a minute to spare. I've told Lena to pack, and now I've got to go and get Meg."

"Meg?"

"Of course. She's coming, too. I shall need her."

"Not to Florence, Clive! You promised that was where we would go."

"And so we shall. We might leave Meg in Rome at that stage. But these are mere details. Now pull yourself together and get dressed."

His voice was curt. Something had happened to make him unnaturally tense and excited. It was the rumor of the picture, of course. He got like that about pictures—much more so than about women.

But he was taking her, wasn't he? She should cling to that straw of pleasure.

"What is the picture?" she remembered to ask.

"It's a genuine Jan de Reeth—or so they think. An unknown old master. Do you realize what that means? If I can get it for a low enough price, our fortune's made."

No wonder he was so excited, Luisa thought. This was the dream that every picture dealer treasured— to discover an unknown old master. But would it be proved genuine after all the extensive tests had been made, the X-rays, the dating of the canvas, the truly old quality of the cracks in the paint, the vivid medieval colors?

"A de Reeth nowadays should fetch at least six figures," Clive said. "It will be a sensation."

"What is it called?"

"Madonna."

He tossed the word into the room as he was leaving. It made Luisa sit very still, thinking. When she and Clive had first met, Clive had taken her face between the palms of his hands. He had looked at it intensely, and said in a low voice, "You have the most perfect madonna face I've ever seen."

But now—Luisa's trembling fingers felt the scars. The madonna quality was unrecognizable, vanished. And Clive had found it in a picture instead. . . .

Lena came bustling in, her face animated to an expression of extreme alarm and disapproval.

"Mrs. Wilton, you're not doing this crazy thing! Flying off to Italy. You're not fit. The doctor will go mad."

"No, he won't, Lena. My husband has telephoned him. He says it's all right. And it will be so wonderful to get away from hospitals for a while. I can wear a veil, Clive says."

"I don't believe the doctor would say any such thing," Lena declared. "Why, you collapse at the least effort. You'll have to be carried off the plane.

It's wicked. And that girl to go, too. Why should I have to pack her things?"

"Oh, Lena, don't be so difficult. Just pack, as you were told to. We haven't much time."

Luisa fiddled with the bracelet round her thin wrist. If they were really going to Florence, did that mean she could stop being so secretive with Meg? Could they go back to the old house together, and recall Grandmamma, and the long long talk the old lady had had with the pretty English girl. Could she be honest at last? Or was Clive up to something else devious?

Lena was pulling open drawers with noisy disapproval.

"Traveling in your condition," she muttered. "It's madness. I don't believe Doctor Lennox would say such a thing. I've a good mind to ring him myself."

"Do, if it will make you happy. Really, Lena, you treat me like a baby."

The woman stopped to give Luisa a long look.

"It's as well you have one person who cares what happens to you, Mrs. Wilton. Even if it's just a plain old fool like me."

Luisa's mouth felt dry.

"What do you mean, Lena?"

"Oh, nothing, nothing! Except that the master will get his own way, won't he?"

"That's impertinent of you, Lena. I should be angry with you."

Luisa was trying to speak calmly. She was thinking of the long time Clive had made her wait before he would buy her so simple a thing as a pretty jingling bracelet that he knew would delight her.

"But if it will ease your mind, Lena, you'd better

ring the doctor. Hear what he says with your own ears."

Lena straightened up.

"I'll do it at once, madam. I meant to, anyway."

She went downstairs to the study, and was away much longer than Luisa could bear. This was treachery to Clive, encouraging even one's servant to have doubts. But she knew that she wasn't really strong enough to travel. The mere thought of the energy required made her feel faint. Even though she told herself that such a longed for trip with a loving husband would be so good for her.

She felt too weak to even begin to dress before Lena came back. And when Lena returned at last, she knew she wasn't going. She had only to see the dark triumph in the older woman's face.

"It's a strange thing to have to tell you, madam, but Doctor Lennox hasn't been talking to your husband today. He says he'd instantly forbid such a crazy idea, anyway. You're not to dream of leaving this house, and he'll be over to see you tomorrow morning."

Luisa gripped the end of the bed.

"Lena, is this true?"

"Now why should I tell you a lie, madam? You know I'd go down on my knees for you. You poor baby! Someone has to look after you and love you."

Luisa's voice was trembling so much that she could scarcely speak.

"What's that piece of paper—you've got—in your hand, Lena?"

"Oh, yes. I found that on his desk. I couldn't help but see it. If things hadn't begun to happen so suddenly he'd never have been so careless as to leave it around. But he got some sort of telephone call that frightened him. That's my guess. Anyway, read this, Mrs. Wilton. Oh, it's not a love letter. Nothing like that. But you mark my words, madam"—and now Lena's words were heavy with drama—"if you and Miss Burney had gone on this trip, neither of you would have come back!"

XIV

Hans frightened Meg by his fierce absorption in his work. His square strong figure hunched over the easel looked as if it hadn't a moment to spare. Occasionally he muttered to himself: "Yes, that's it, that's it. The winged look, the flying look. Lift your chin, girl. No, not as much as that. That's better. And think of something pleasant. You have pleasant things to think of, surely."

The perspiration stood out on his forehead. His face was sculptured into deep lines. Why, with his sick friend in Holland, and with his worry about Miss Burt (because he was deeply worried—that faked telephone call had shaken him badly) did he insist on continuing with the portrait? And why this curtness to her, as if she were a stranger? If Simon hadn't told her it was important, she couldn't have stayed. Although now she was as determined as Simon to find out what went on.

"When can I see what you've done, Hans?"

He didn't look up. "Probably never."

"Oh, but after giving you my spare time—"

"I told you you would only see it if it was good enough," he snapped.

Sheer nervousness made Meg go on talking.

"But if you're going away tomorrow, how will I ever know if it was good enough?"

"Oh, you women! Pry, pry, pry! What I paint is entirely my own business. Now what in heavens' name are you doing?"

"I'm going," said Meg with dignity. "I came here to do you a favor, not to listen to you being rude to me."

Hans advanced placatingly, a smile uneasily on his thunderous face.

"Now, Meg, Meg! Don't take offense. I know I'm irritable today. I have a great many worries. But I must finish this. It's important. If only you knew how important it is."

Meg sat down reluctantly. She was remembering again that Simon had told her to stay.

"Then only until Simon comes."

"Oh, yes, your young man. Why must he come here for you? Does he think you're in danger? From me?" He spread out his hands exasperatedly. "I'm only dangerous, I might tell you, when my work is threatened. So sit still, please. You will be quite safe."

For the first time it occurred to Meg that Janie might have run away because she was frightened. And that might be the message she had intended Meg to get from her note.

She began to listen with considerable eagerness for the doorbell.

Instead of the doorbell, however, it was the telephone which rang.

In spite of his absorption in his work, Hans must have been listening just as eagerly for the telephone as she had been for the doorbell. He flung down his brush with a muttered, "Good!" and hurried from the room.

Meg didn't feel that her former promise not to attempt to see Hans' work until it was finished counted any longer. She crossed the room and stood in front of the easel.

She saw with perplexity that Hans had not yet started on her portrait. He had merely been making several studies of her head. The first ones were faithful likenesses of her as she sat in her linen dress, with her hair smooth and her lips smiling. But the unfinished one today was entirely different. It was meant, obviously to be the head of an angel. It floated in clouds, radiance streaming from it. The sweet downcast eyes, the smiling lips, the airy floating quality of it were exquisite. Even in its first rough state it was the work of a master.

She had meant to take only a quick look and return to her seat, but surprise made her stay there gazing with mingled pleasure and incredulity. She didn't even hear Hans return until his voice said softly, "So!"

Meg started guiltily.

"I looked," she said. Then her enthusiasm overcame her nervousness.

"It's wonderful! You never told me you could paint like this."

He was close beside her looking down at her with his fierce, brooding gaze. His fingers were circled loosely around her arm. She could hear his heavy breathing. She was rigid. It seemed that he as about to attack her for her disobedience. She wasn't supposed to have looked at the painting. Now she had stumbled on some important secret, the meaning of which she couldn't yet interpret.

Silently she measured the distance to the door. Would he seize her if she tried to run? Would he remember in this moment of anger that Simon was due to arrive at any moment?

She made a tentative movement, and the strong fingers round her arm tightened warningly.

But all Hans said, still in his deceptively soft voice was, "You like it?"

Meg managed to answer calmly, "It's like something out of the Uffizi. A Botticelli angel."

"Not a Botticelli! A Hans Cromer. Yes, now you have seen it, you might as well know."

His voice was harsh with pride and triumph. His grip loosened. Meg realized that appreciation of his work was the way to diminish the knotted anger within him. She made herself go on talking enthusiastically.

"But, Hans, if you can work like this you're not a bad artist at all. You're great."

"Of course I'm a great artist," he said impatiently. "It only remains for the world to recognize it. And it will. I promise you it will."

Meg was beginning to relax a little as certain perplexities became clear.

"So that's why Clive backed you. He knows."

Hans shrugged.

"Clive is an astute business man. But let's get back to work. There's no time, no time at all."

He gave her a push towards her seat. Meg realized that she must obey. Now that he was calmer it wouldn't be wise to antagonize him again. When he became absorbed in his work perhaps she could seize an opportunity and slip past him to the door. Anyway, Simon should be here any moment. If Hans could just be kept calm until then. . . .

"Did you do just as good a painting of Janie? Did she see it?"

"She saw it. She thought it was terrible. She hadn't your perception."

"In that glorious dress?" Meg asked.

"She thought she looked medieval and shrewish."

"And Luisa?" asked Meg, and then stopped, her breath caught.

There was some fact she could recognize. If Hans had done such an exquisite painting of Luisa, it should never have been hidden away, or destroyed.

But perhaps it had not been destroyed. Perhaps it was Luisa who had been, instead. . . .

"That was Clive on the telephone a moment ago," Hans was saying, as if he had read her thoughts. "He wants you to go home at once. But I said I must keep you a little longer."

"Why does he want me?"

"It appears he has had some unexpected information about a painting he covets very much. He may be able to get it if he goes to Italy immediately. But I told him fifteen minutes one way or the other isn't going to make too much difference."

"To . . . Italy?" Meg was still finding it difficult to breathe.

"He's going to take you. And Luisa."

"Luisa, too?"

Hans was watching her beneath lowered eyelids. His eyes were shining darkly.

"To Florence," he said slyly.

"No!" Meg sprang up. "No! That can't be true."

"It is true. And you must go. I don't think Clive will let you refuse. He's a man who gets his own way. Anyway, think what a wonderful trip for you —you with your rare appreciation of masterpieces."

She couldn't stand the way he was looking at her, his face carved into ridges, his eyes full of that menacing brightness. . . .

Again she measured the distance to the door. Would he let her go?

"Hans, if you don't mind—I think I ought to go. Mr. Wilton doesn't like to be kept waiting. After all,"—she tried to speak lightly—"I am still his secretary."

"He can wait." Hans had picked up his brush again.

"But—"

"He isn't the master forever," Hans said inexplicably. "I will show him. Sit down. Stay where you are."

Meg, on her feet, stood uncertainly.

"Sit down." She recognized the soft but deadly command in his voice. "Do you want me to make you, the way I did the others?"

"What—others?"

"You know very well, little one. You're not stupid. Not stupid enough, unfortunately. And I may appear to be soft and foolish, but that is deceptive. Sit down again."

Meg's trembling legs forced her to obey.

"Hans, please let me go."

"When I'm ready."

"Then did you keep the others, Janie and Luisa, here against their will, too?"

"No. Only the old lady." Hans was working feverishly. He didn't look up. His words had been quite casual. It seemed as if he had said them without thinking, unwittingly dropping the grim information.

"The old lady! You mean . . ." and now Meg could no longer hide her terror, ". . . Miss Burt?"

Hans looked up, suddenly bland.

"Miss Burt? Whatever are you talking about. Would I want to paint that old ragbag? You're talking too much, my dear. Just stay still—"

But at that moment the doorbell rang, and Meg sprang up in exquisite relief.

"That will be Simon! Thank heaven!"

Hans made one furious exclamation. Then he controlled himself.

"Don't be in such a hurry, Meg. It's not very complimentary to me. Anyway, it may not be your boyfriend. It may even be the postman."

Meg didn't intend to wait for Hans to find out who it was. Seizing the opportunity of his relaxed attention, she had slipped past him, and was through the door and down the narrow stairs before he could stop her.

"Si—"

In the fading light, Clive stood on the doorstep, smiling.

"I've come for you, Meg. We haven't much time. Didn't Hans tell you?"

He looked so normal and friendly that Meg wondered what all her wild fears had been about. It was Hans' house that did this to her. Its queer sinister atmosphere plunged her into complete unreality.

"I'm glad to see you, Mr. Wilton. Hans has been scaring me stiff."

Clive darted a quick look at Hans.

"Have you, you old devil. Don't worry about him, Meg. I should have warned you. He lives in a constant state of melodrama. But come along now."

"I can't, I'm sorry. Simon's calling for me."

The geniality went out of Clive's face.

"Do you work for Simon?"

"No, but—"

"Then come along. Hans will give him a message. Or you can ring him from my house, if you must. But if you want my advice, you'll forget him."

"Why?" she asked sharply.

"Don't ask me to explain just now. I should have warned you about him, too. But there's no time. And anyway, it doesn't matter. Things have been happening unexpectedly, and we have a plane to catch. Lena's packing. I told her to pack your things, too."

Meg's brain was whirling. She stuck stubbornly to the first point.

"What about Simon?"

"Do you really think he makes a living from that dusty shop? Hans could tell you—but Meg, really, there isn't time. We'll talk on the plane. Don't you want to come? I need you to look after Luisa and to help me. I'd like you to see this picture, too. Its discovery has quite a romance attached to it. You'll enjoy it."

Meg felt dizzy. Too much had happened in the last half hour. She couldn't help feeling that somehow it all connected—the discovery of Hans' true ability, Simon's strange insistence that she go to his house and sit for him, and now this sudden trip to Italy.

Who was she to trust? Simon? Hans? Clive? Or none of them. The only clear thoughts in her mind were that she had to get away from Hans' house, and that she couldn't go anywhere, to Italy or even to London, without telling Simon. And if he advised her not to go she would listen to him. It came to her that she was always going to listen to Simon, seriously and devotedly, no matter what Clive or anyone else might try to tell her.

"It's impossible to go at a moment's notice like this," she said confusedly.

"It's not impossible at all, Meg." Clive's monkeyish face was gentle, persuasive, full of affection and kindness. "The only impossible thing would be not to come."

XV

Mrs. Martin from the Crown came rushing into Simon's shop.

"There you are at last, Mr. Somers. Oh, I'm sorry, I didn't notice you had a customer."

In the gloom, the rather stout form of the woman in black wasn't at first noticeable.

"That's all right," said Simon. "She'll wait a minute. What is it?"

"There's a phone call for you."

"For me?"

"It's that Janie Howard. She said she'd been trying to get you at the shop, but couldn't get an answer. It's urgent, she says."

Simon leapt for the door.

"I've just come in. Is she waiting?"

"Good gracious! Are you just leaving your customer like that?" Mrs. Martin exclaimed. "It's the telephone in the bar. You are in a hurry, aren't you? I didn't know you were that fond of Janie."

"At this moment," said Simon, "I could kiss her. You see, I thought she might be dead."

As they went, something moved in the darkness of Simon's shop.

"Cor," said the police sergeant, mopping his brow. "What a game!"

But the stout woman in black standing facing him didn't answer. Neither did she move.

Meg returned to the house with Clive because it seemed the only thing to do to escape Hans, since Simon hadn't come. She had watched Hans helplessly fuming while Clive made all the plans. She had almost been sorry for him. He could bluster to a woman but with a man, or with Clive at least, he was once more ignominiously deflated.

There were a great many things to be explained, but the first thing was to get out of Hans' house, and the next to ring Simon.

Clive hurried her home so fast that she was out of breath, and almost as confused as when she had started. But not quite as confused. She had decided to refuse to go to Italy without first discussing it with Simon. It was fantastic to just go off like that without telling anyone. Clive suggested sending postcards from Rome and surprising everyone.

"Where's your spirit of adventure?" he asked, and Meg knew that a week ago, before this tangle of strange events, she would have done precisely what he suggested.

"We'll talk on the plane," he said. "Yes, about Hans, too. Of course I've known for a long time that he has these flashes of amazing talent. It's as if he has some sort of mental block, and only now and again the message gets through to his brain."

"I thought he might have been deliberately concealing his ability," Meg said.

Clive gave her a quick sideways look.

"Why should he conceal what he longs to have recognized? I doubt very much if he's capable of the sustained effort of a major painting. But he's interesting. Very interesting. We'll see what happens. That's why I do what I can for him. I hope, by the way, he didn't frighten you. He gets very intense."

"He did," said Meg simply. "I want to know a lot more about all this before I go away with you and Luisa."

Clive patted her shoulder.

"You shall know all there is to know, my dear. None of it's in the least alarming. But let's hurry now. We must leave in less than an hour."

They couldn't force her to go, Meg reassured herself. At the moment all she had to do was get back to Clive's house and ring Simon. But supposing Simon wasn't at his shop. . . . Supposing. . . .

"Where are you going, Meg?" Clive's quiet voice came behind her, as, in the house, she was making for the telephone. "There's no time for you to make any telephone calls. I want you to help Luisa. You can ring anyone you have to from the airport."

Meg realized the underlying command in his mild voice. It flashed through her mind that, in his own way, he might be more dangerous than Hans. . . . She shrugged off the thought.

"It won't take a minute—" If she could get Simon immediately, and he would come. . . .

"Do you want me to lose this picture? The opportunity of a lifetime? Don't you realize that every minute counts."

He sounded so deadly serious that Meg hesitated. Supposing he were really telling the truth. If there were such a picture as he described she would be as eager as he to be in on the find. It would be awful to spoil it for him.

"Who is the artist?" she asked uncertainly.

"Jan de Reeth."

"No! But that's fabulous. You mean an unknown picture?"

"If it's genuine. And my very reliable spies tell me it is." Clive was smiling. "There, I can see this makes you look at things differently."

"But where was it discovered?"

"I can tell you that," came Luisa's composed voice from the stairs.

"Luisa!" Clive had gone rigid. Meg saw the hard fury distort his face.

"No, Clive, don't stop me! It's too late to do so, anyway. I've read your notes." Luisa stood halfway down the stairs. She held her head very high and proudly. With her back to the light, the slight twisting and scarring of her face was scarcely noticeable. She had the air of a young proud beauty—of the budding beauty Meg had seen in the girl in the Florentine villa.

"The picture isn't discovered yet, Meg. It's still to be discovered. In my old family villa outside Florence."

"You *are* Angelica!" Meg whispered.

Luisa touched her marred face fleetingly.

"Luisa Angelica, yes. For business reasons my husband wanted that kept a secret. But now you can be told, since the famous de Reeth is to be discovered in the wreckage of my home. Perhaps it isn't even an impossible story," she went on. "In the past, members of my family were patrons of the arts. In spite of the war, some dusty old paintings in need of restoring may have been hidden in attics and escaped looting."

"But the house is in ruins," Meg exclaimed. "I saw it."

"That doesn't deter my husband," said Luisa calmly. "Listen to what he has already prepared to give the newspapers."

Clive made a sharp movement, but Luisa, with her new air of authority, calmly read:

"London art dealer discovers what is thought to be an authentic old master in the moldering ruins of Italian villa. Clive Wilton is convinced he has found a genuine Jan de Reeth; the famous seventeenth century Dutch painting is one of the finest examples of de Reeth's art, and its value is inestimable. The subject is the Madonna with attendant angels, and, in the foreground, the figure of a woman in the dress of the period. This figure, according to de Reeth's custom of putting his current wife into his paintings, is probably that of his fourth wife. The events leading to the discovery of the picture are almost as romantic as the picture itself, as two years ago Clive Wilton married the beautiful young Italian girl who is the sole surviving member of the Sigroni family to whom the villa belonged."

Luisa ceased reading, and looked down at her husband.

"But you haven't finished this little fantasy, my darling. You haven't told your adoring public what happened to the beautiful young girl you married? They'll want to know, I'm sure."

Meg had run up the stairs to seize Luisa's arm.

"Who is the Madonna in the picture?" She realized she was shouting. "Who is she?"

Luisa smiled tightly.

"Clive will tell you she's an ancestor of mine. That will explain the likeness to anyone who may—remember me." Her voice faltered at last, and Meg, grasping her arm in horror, heard Clive say quite gently, "That's enough of the drama. Now you girls get ready."

Meg slipped her arm protectively round Luisa's waist. She could feel the girl trembling, and realized that she had used up all her strength in that act of defiance.

"Mr. Wilton, do you really think we'll go, after that?" Her voice was full of scorn. She was no longer afraid. If Luisa could show so much courage, so could she. "Luisa's face is ruined, Janie disappears, and I, I the angel—what am I to expect to happen to me?"

"You're still unharmed, Meg. And you'll stay that way only if you obey me." Clive had made a neat unobtrusive movement, and taken a revolver from his hip pocket. "I'm not going to hurt anybody. I hope I won't have to. I just intend you to do as I tell you."

"We'll never come back," Meg whispered. "We all know too much."

"You must blame my wife for that. She's the one who pried in my desk."

"And you're the one who's in too much of a hurry!" Meg jumped as Lena's strident voice rang out behind her. "Oh, yes, Mr. Wilton, it's you who's made the mistake. You couldn't resist putting your plot into words—all too soon. You wife didn't pry in your desk, I did. And if you're going to shoot her, it will be over my dead body."

The grim-faced old woman had come from up-stairs to stand in front of Luisa.

Clive sighed with exaggerated patience.

"So you're in it, too, Lena. I thought you'd have more sense. If you'd only understand that no one is to be killed. You're all to simply keep your mouths shut and do as I say."

"As *you* say!" exclaimed Lena in her terrible accusing voice. "When you worked out this whole devilish plot before you married this innocent girl. Oh, I mightn't be educated, but I've seen what's going on. You tried to kill her when you didn't need her any longer."

"That was an accident!" Clive rapped.

"And lucky for you, it disfigured her face, which was the important thing. Don't think we don't all know in Frenchley that it was very strange you could jump clear from the car, and knew the exact moment to do it."

Clive's face had gone very pale. He didn't have Hans' dark menacing look. He was a neat slim conventional man suddenly indescribably deadly.

"I can't risk missing that plane. So get moving." His voice was cut and harsh. "As for you, Lena, you old fool, you're not the only one who pried too much. There was another, as Hans will tell you—"

He didn't finish his sentence, for at that moment the doorbell rang.

That was when he showed his first sign of panic. Meg saw the whites of his eyes flash, then he said in a low rapid voice, "If there's the faintest sound out of anyone—"

They stood, scarcely breathing. Would whoever was there go away, innocently supposing no one was home? Meg was tense with silent prayer. Let it be Simon! Let him peer inquisitively through the windows.

The bell rang again, loud and insistently. Lena made a sudden movement. As Clive lifted his hand to check her Hans' voice came hoarsely, "Clive! Clive! Open the door."

Like magic, Clive's face cleared.

"You damned fool, why didn't you say who it was?"

He strode across the hall to the door. "What are you doing, running up here again like a scared rabbit? I told you to get away—" Again his words were cut off.

For the open door showed, not Hans' square form, but that of a stout woman in a shabby black coat and an old shapeless hat. She swayed a little towards Clive, and then, as he stepped back in gray-faced horror, gently collapsed into his arms.

That was when his nerve broke. Violently he pushed the figure away, as if his whole body were rigid with disgust.

"Hans, what sort of a diabolical trick is this? You know the crazy old woman's dead."

"Yes. Four days ago, to be precise," came Simon's voice, and there was Simon standing behind the bowed figure of Hans. "You helped bury her, didn't you, Clive? You took your car out late at night and went to Hans' cottage the back way, across the railway line. When you hoped none of the neighbors would notice something had been rolled down the embankment for removal."

"Hans, you traitor!" said Clive thickly.

Simon stepped into the hall, casually pushing aside the dressmaker's dummy that had already lost its makeshift hat. Hans was behind him, and behind him again two policemen.

"They made me do it, Clive," he whimpered. "They broke into my house. They saw the picture. They've ruined my life's work."

"Your life's work!" Clive said in a highly hysterical voice. "What about mine! And it's all your crazy fault. You must have the face of an angel, you said! There would be no more risk than with the others. But from then on"—he turned to give Meg a look of blazing hatred—"that lovely angel face, those innocent blue eyes that wouldn't have the intelligence to see anything odd—"

"That will be enough!" Simon rapped.

One of the police stepped forward ponderously.

"I have a warrant here for your arrest, Mr. Wilton. It's my duty to warn you that anything you say may be used in evidence against you."

"Clive!" cried Luisa faintly, and collapsed into Lena's arms.

She had fainted. She was unaware that her husband left the house without a single glance in the direction of his adoring and beautiful young Italian bride.

XVI

Meg felt like death herself. It was quite a time before the stairs and the hall and the open front door, now framing only the sweet spring twilight, stopped swaying dizzily.

"Lena, we must get her to bed."

"Yes, madam. Oh, thank heaven, madam, that wicked villain has gone. I always suspected him. That's why I stayed on here. I never would have otherwise. But someone had to protect this poor innocent child. I knew the day would come when she needed me badly. I'll go on looking after her if she'll let me."

"We'll all look after her," said Meg unsteadily. "Won't we, Simon?"

Simon bent over Luisa's limp body.

"She'll be all right," he said gently. "She's young. She may even forget. Let me carry her upstairs."

When they had settled Luisa in bed and left her in Lena's care, Meg clutched Simon's arm. She was finding it difficult now not to weep.

"Oh, Simon, we were nearly on our way to Italy. Even I was almost convinced that there really was such a picture."

"So there is, almost."

"And is Miss Burt really dead?"

"All too evidently. For several days."

"But she was in her room. I heard her walking about."

"That, I imagine, was the devious Clive. It was necessary to keep up the fiction for a little while that Miss Burt was in the house, so Clive slipped in the back way while you were there, and took in the tea tray and so on. Hans, of course fed the birds on the window-sill for the benefit of any neighbors watching. And the form in the window was what Janie discovered one evening. A dressmaker's dummy dressed in the old lady's clothes, again for the benefit of inquisitive neighbors. Janie was so frightened she was going to call the police. But Hans persuaded her not to. He convinced her that Miss Burt was safe in an old women's home, and if Janie would go away and wait for him, he could come and marry her as soon as he had finished something he was doing. He told her he was just on the verge of making a nice sum of money."

"How do you know all this?"

"Janie rang me half an hour ago and tied up all the loose ends. She said Hans was crazy about her and couldn't bear hurting her, so he took the risk of trusting her. But poor silly loyal Janie got worrying about you. She was afraid you might find out something, too, and Hans might not be quite so kind. Anyway, she'd discovered that she couldn't love a man who did such eccentric things."

"Then what did—happen to Miss Burt?" Meg asked reluctantly.

"She discovered Hans' carefully guarded secret. He was working on a painting that was later to be planted in Luisa's old home in Florence and discovered. You remember those old frames I found for Clive? He didn't want the frames at all, but the canvases, which could be cleaned and used again so that the age would be authentic. Had you discovered yet that Hans is a wonderful artist?"

"Yes, I had. Just today," Meg said reminiscently.

"Well, Clive had discovered this, too. The only drawback was that Hans insisted on having real life models with which to create his masterpiece. He made numerous sketches of them in his studio and later, when alone, worked on the real canvas. His pose as a bad artist was merely to put everyone off the scent. He used to hide the picture in the little room at the top of the house from which stairs led straight down to the basement. He usually kept the door of this room locked, but one day he was careless and Miss Burt was inquisitive. Anyway, there she was gazing at the half-finished canvas and exclaiming that there was Mrs. Wilton, and wasn't she beautiful, all in blue like a madonna. Hans got in a panic and grabbed her by the throat and she fell down the stairs. All the way to the bottom. She broke her neck. Then he didn't know what to do with the body. He couldn't say it had been an accident, because he has very strong fingers, and the old lady's throat was badly marked. So he got in a panic and called in Clive. Said he'd talk about the whole scheme if he didn't help."

"That was the night Clive drove the car!"

"Yes. They went out to Dungeness and buried the poor old creature in the strip of wasteland that's marked dangerous because of unexploded mines."

"Perhaps it's a pity they didn't step on a mine. Then a bit of their beauty might have been destroyed." Meg was unashamedly vindictive. "But how utterly stupid they were. Because then Hans had to get what everyone thought was the real Miss Burt away."

"Which he did, later, when Janie had given him that fright. He didn't dare to take any more risks."

Meg thought of the dark house, and the atmosphere of menace which she thought she must have imagined.

"You let me go back there," she accused.

"I had to. But I knew you were safe as long as Hans was working. As soon as I discovered the telephone trick had worked and that Clive was in a flap as well as Hans, I knew what to do. Meg, I can't say how sorry I am for that bad half hour you had, or how I worried about you. But this seemed to be the only way."

Meg gave him a shaky smile. "I wouldn't have been allowed to come back from Italy, would I? I knew too much. Luisa being Angelica, for instance. I suppose I might not have recognized myself in the angel faces, but I'd have been one of the very few people who would have recognized Luisa as she used to be. What a cold-blooded plot it was. And yet I could have been certain Clive loved Luisa in his own way."

"Not him. He isn't capable of love. He's much too ambitious."

"Is the picture really that good?"

"If you can bear it," said Simon, "you must see it. Its a masterpiece. Hans knows his stuff. He could mix the old colors, those wonderful heavenly blues, for instance. And he knew all the detail about cleaning the original picture from a genuinely old canvas, and painting in the age cracks. Certainly this picture might have been proved a fake eventually, but I believe Hans might have got away with it, just as that chap who did the Vermeers did. Having Luisa's home as an authentic background to make the discovery was one of the greatest assets. As for Hans himself, he's full of resentment that he's never been acknowledged as a great artist. The war and other things conspired against him. So he decided deliberately to prove that he could do as well as one of his ancestors. He says he's legitimately descended from the famous Jan de Reeth. Indeed, I suspect he thinks he is Jan de Reeth reincarnated. He's suffering from delusions."

There was still something that puzzled Meg.

"But Luisa must have suspected there was something odd going on. Why didn't she tell anyone? Was she really so loyal to Clive?"

Lena had come into the room and stood listening. It was she who answered Meg's question.

"I can tell you why she said nothing. The poor child had a weakness. She stole pretty things, mostly jewelry. Who can blame her, she was so starved as a child. But her husband, the devil used that in his own favor. He told her dreadful things the British police would do for such a crime, but he wouldn't say a word as long as she always obeyed him. He terrorized her; that's the long and the short of it."

"Yet she still took things?" Meg asked.

"Only occasionally. I don't think she could help it. They say kleptomaniacs don't know they're doing it."

"And all this for that terrible picture," Meg said.

"It's a beautiful picture," Simon pointed out. "Beautiful, but imperfect. It still has to have the angel's face. And that's never going to happen because"—he put his hands lightly on her cheeks—"it's mine now, and I refuse permission."

Tears trembled on Meg's lashes.

"Simon, he really could paint exquisitely. I saw."

"Darling, if you're going to cry, put your head on my shoulder. If it comes to that, if we're going to give Hans his due, I've also got to thank Clive for bringing you here. But they're a pair of deadly megalomaniacs, the two of them. They deserve all they're going to get."

His arm tighted round Meg. She felt the knotted tension inside herself easing, and knew a moment of strange warm bliss.

"Simon—do you know what would make me feel better?"

"If I kissed you?"

"If I could come to your shop and polish some of

that lovely old silver and brass. It would make me very happy and peaceful."

His embrace was painful and infinitely satisfying.

"Bless you, Meg. You've got yourself a lifetime job."

DORIS MILES DISNEY

*13928 **The Day Miss Bessie Lewis Disappeared** $1.50

*32270 **Heavy, Heavy Hangs** $1.50

*48990 **Look Back on Murder** $1.75

80790 **Three's A Crowd** $1.25

*83370 **Two Little Children And How They Grew** $1.50

*88590 **Who Rides a Tiger** 95c

The Novels of
Dorothy Eden

$1.75 each

07931	Bride by Candlelight
07977	Bridge of Fear
*08184	The Brooding Lake
*09257	Cat's Prey
*12354	Crow Hollow
*13884	The Daughters of Ardmore Hall
*14184	The Deadly Travelers
*14187	Death Is A Red Rose
*22543	Face Of An Angel
*47404	The Laughing Ghost
*48479	Listen To Danger
*57804	The Night of the Letter
*67854	The Pretty Ones
*76073	Shadow of a Witch
*76972	Sleep in the Woods
*77125	The Sleeping Bride
*86598	Voice of the Dolls
*88533	Whistle for the Crows
$94393	Yellow Is For Fear and Other Stories

Available wherever paperbacks are sold or use this coupon.

ace books, (Dept. MM) Box 576, Times Square Station
New York, N.Y. 10036
Please send me titles checked above.

I enclose $.................Add 35c handling fee per copy.

Name ....

Address ....

City...................... State.............. Zip.........